THE BEACH HOUSE

RACHEL HANNA

CHAPTER 1

*S*he stood at the breakfast bar and looked out over her large home, now emptier than it had ever been. A part of her life was now behind her; the one where little children were underfoot, softball games were every weekend and first dates had come and gone. Now, she and her husband were empty nesters.

"Miss Julie, is there anything else I can do for you today?" her housekeeper, Agnes, asked. Agnes had been cleaning her house since her daughters were knee high to a grasshopper, as her grandmother would say.

"No, but thank you, Aggie. Head on home and put your feet up!"

Agnes smiled gratefully as Julie handed her an envelope with her final paycheck, plus a dash extra.

"I wish I could take you to the new beach house with us, but the place just isn't big enough to need a housekeeper. I guess I'll have to learn to do it myself," Julie said with a sad laugh. It truly was the end of an era in so many ways.

"I know this place will make another family a great home," Agnes said, looking around. Julie hoped the older woman would finally retire, although she said cleaning was her hobby and she might as well get paid for it.

Julie looked around also. Memories were housed in every nook and cranny, from the corner where they always put the Christmas tree to the gouge in the molding where their old Great Dane had slid across the hardwood floors chasing after a ball and crashed into the wall.

Memories were good and bad. Her eyes started to mist, which was not something she enjoyed, so she quickly changed the subject.

"Thank you for getting this place so clean. Our real estate agent already has three families interested, so I don't think we'll even have to put a sign in the yard! One of them has already made an offer, in fact."

Agnes smiled. "I'll miss you. Please tell the girls I love them and to send me a postcard, okay?"

Julie pulled her into an embrace. "You know they love you like a grandmother, Aggie. They'll keep in touch. I promise."

Julie was so proud of her daughters. Now both adults, they were taking the world by storm. Her nineteen-year old daughter, Meg, was studying abroad in France for another year, and Colleen, her twenty-year old, was at college across the country in California. She had a prestigious internship at a law firm out there, so she rarely came home for a visit.

That just left Julie and her husband of twenty-one years, Michael. For as long as she could remember, she'd had one dream that never died - to buy a little beach cottage along the South Carolina coast and enjoy their empty nest years while they were still young.

At only forty-three years old, Julie didn't consider herself retired. Quite the contrary, in fact. She ran a popular online boutique, and she would continue to do so from her new beach house. In fact, she and Michael had put a contract on a place months ago, and the wonderful sellers had agreed to wait for them to get their house sold and tie up loose ends. The closing was coming up in a couple of weeks, and Michael had just enough time to go on one last business trip before officially retiring from his sales job.

Once they moved, he'd be starting his own business too, and her dreams of them being beach bums in their forties would finally come true. Julie could hardly wait.

The beach was her happy place. The constant ebbing and flowing of the water gave her a peace she couldn't explain in words, and the house they were buying sat right at the water's edge. She often imagined what it would be like to sip her morning coffee while watching the dolphins swim by, and soon that would be her reality. She could hardly contain her excitement.

Michael wasn't as big a fan of the beach, but he'd always let her dream and gone along with what she wanted. She was the one always reaching for the stars, but Michael had always been more of the worker bee type, never really dreaming much past the present moment. Still, he'd succeeded in his job so well that they'd lived a pretty luxurious life, and Julie was thankful for that. Although her boutique brought in money, it was nowhere near enough to support them without Michael's income.

When the girls had both left home, there'd been a year of what almost felt like shock for the both of them. The house was quiet. Gone were the days of dozens of kids packing their house on the weekends, with loud sleepovers and dance parties til three AM.

They'd complained about it at the time, but when it was gone, the silence had been deafening. It took a few months before Michael, especially, had seemed back to normal. They developed new routines, like having breakfast on their patio together before he left for work. And, all the while, Agnes had continued making their house pretty and clean even though there wasn't really anyone there to mess it up anymore.

As Julie stood in the big front window overlooking her driveway, she watched Agnes pull away in her small compact car and through the gates of her wealthy neighborhood. Yes, they'd been so blessed financially over the years, but now they were blessed in a different kind of way. With love. With a strong marriage that had stood the test of time. With a new start in a whole new place, away from the hustle and bustle of suburban Atlanta.

Julie smiled at the thought of it. Her dreams were all about to come true.

~

IT WAS ALMOST SEVEN O'CLOCK, and Michael still wasn't home. His plane had landed at four, and she'd even looked online to make sure it landed safely. She'd called his co-worker who was on the trip too, but Marc had made it home over an hour ago, even with the crazy Atlanta traffic.

Where was Michael?

She'd tried texting him, but no response. Calls went straight to voicemail. She was getting more worried by the minute. Should she call the police? Was she overreacting?

Just as she was about to dial 911, she heard the garage door open. Out of the window, she saw the tail end of his black BMW pulling into the side garage. A mixture of relief and outright anger flowed through her veins. Why was he late, and why hadn't he answered her numerous texts and calls?

"Thank God you're okay!" she said when he finally walked through the door. He wasn't wearing his normal business suit; instead, he was in khaki shorts, a pale pink polo shirt and boat shoes. He never wore that sort of thing on a business trip, even on the plane ride back.

"Why wouldn't I be okay?" he said, a certain level of irritation in his voice. He didn't look at her as he walked in and rolled his one piece of luggage into the corner.

"Your plane landed hours ago, and I've been texting you. And calling. Why didn't you answer?"

"You're overreacting, Julie. I was driving. You know I don't mess with my phone while I'm driving. Remember Kit?"

He often referred to his old friend, Kit, who was killed in a car accident years ago by a distracted teenage driver. Still, it normally didn't take him over three hours to get home.

"Was traffic bad? Because Marc made it home an hour ago." She was getting more and more dubious about his answers, and he still wasn't making eye contact.

He looked at her, his face turning red from anger. "Seriously? You called Marc? Are you trying to make me look like an idiot at work?"

"Michael, I was worried! I was about to call the police!"

"Oh my gosh… get a grip, Julie! I was a little late. It's not the end of the world, okay?" He stormed down the hall to their bedroom and sat down in the chair to take off his shoes.

Something was off. His demeanor had never been like this. Michael wasn't one to even raise his voice, which had made her the prime disciplinarian of their girls over the years. She was always the "bad guy" and he got to play the "good guy" role.

"And why would you care what Marc or people at work think? This was your last trip, right? I mean, we are moving to the beach in a few weeks…"

He froze in place. The silence in the room was deafening, and for a moment she thought her ears had stopped working. He wouldn't look at her again.

"Michael? Has something happened?"

"I don't want to do this tonight, Julie. I'm tired. It was a long trip." He stood up and walked to the closet, staring at his side of the large closet for a few moments before turning to her.

"What? You're freaking me out. Tell me what's wrong. I can help you, honey," she said, reaching out to touch his shoulder. He pulled away.

"I'm moving out."

"I know. We both are, sweetie. To our new beach house. Everything will be wonderful there."

"No. Julie, you're not listening. I'm... leaving you."

She stopped breathing. The heartbeat in her head was like a pounding jackhammer. The room started to spin a bit as she tried to get her equilibrium again. She grabbed the handle of the closet door and struggled to suck in a deep breath.

"What?"

"There's... someone else."

Someone else? How could there be someone else? They had a good marriage. A happy life. Two girls. A maid. A new beach house. Maybe he was drinking? Or someone had slipped him a drug on the plane?

"This can't be happening..." she stammered. "Who? Why?"

Michael sighed. "Does it matter, Jules?"

"First of all, don't call me that! Cheaters don't get to call me that!" Now she was angry. She walked toward him, her finger pointed at his face, rage literally coursing through her veins like waves after a hurricane. "And second, yes it matters! I want to know who the home wrecker is!"

He walked past her and back into the bedroom before sitting in the chair again. He covered his face and leaned back. "I really didn't want to do this tonight," he repeated.

She followed him out and stood in front of the chair. "Oh, I'm sorry. I know you must be tired. Would you rather crush my heart and smash all of my dreams tomorrow then? What time shall I pencil you into my calendar to be a gigantic cheating jackass? Is lunchtime good for you? No? Might mess with your digestion... I know how you get constipated easily... Have you told your hussy that little tidbit about yourself?"

"Enough, Julie! I never meant for this to happen!" he said, standing up. "It just...."

"Happened? Yeah, I hear a lot of cheaters say that on those trashy daytime talk shows. Unfortunately, that's a crock and you know it! You made a decision, Michael! At least give me the respect of telling me who... and how... this happened."

He sucked in sharply and sat back down. Julie calmed herself enough to sit on the bed a few feet away, preparing herself to hear the gory details she never thought she'd hear.

"Her name is Victoria. She lives in Boston."

All of those business trips to Boston... Now it made more sense.

"So these business trips were all fake?" Her heart hurt as she felt the first of the unwanted tears dripping down her face.

"Not all of them. At first, I was there to set up our new division. One night, after a particularly crappy meeting, I went to a restaurant. They didn't have seating for one. I sat at the bar. Then this woman came in..."

"Good Lord, this is unbelievable."

"You can't help who you fall in love with, Julie."

She stood up again. "Seriously? You were supposed to be in love with me, Michael! Me! Your wife of twenty-one years! The mother of your two daughters! Was that all fake too?"

"Of course not! I loved you!"

"Past tense? Really?"

He sighed again. "Victoria just gets me. And there's something else…"

"There's more? Lovely."

"We have a six month old son. His name is Charlie."

Once again, she couldn't breathe. Michael had always wanted a son, but after two difficult pregnancies, Julie had said no more. That had created a huge rift in their marriage for years, but they'd eventually gotten past it. Now, he had his son and his perky-bosomed soulmate. She wanted to vomit.

"How could you? So you've been living this secret life where you go to Boston a couple of times a month and spend time with your other family? Dear God, what are Meg and Colleen going to think of this?"

"You can't tell them."

"Have you fallen and hit your head? They have to know they have a little brother!"

"I just mean, let me tell them. Please."

She sat down and pushed back her tears. "Fine. Spin it however you want, but good luck. Your daughters aren't idiots like me. They'll smell your lies a mile away."

"Julie, I never meant to hurt you. But life is short, and I want to be happy again."

"I was the fool who thought I made you happy all these years."

"You did… for a long time."

"Wow. Well, sorry I didn't make the cut for the second half of your life. I guess I'm not young and hot enough anymore."

"Julie, she's only a year younger than you are. It's not like that."

Well, that was a punch to the gut. She couldn't even blame

this on a younger, hotter woman. Nope. She just wasn't enough all the way around.

"I have a flight leaving tomorrow, and I'll send movers for my things next week. I spoke to the real estate agent yesterday, and our counter offer was accepted so the buyers will close in three weeks."

"And where am I supposed to go, Michael?"

"I wasn't going to leave you in the lurch, Julie. You might think I'm a horrible person right now, and I do too, honestly."

"Not enough, apparently. You're still going to Boston."

"I have to go. My son is there, and seeing him off and on isn't good for his development."

"I don't even know what to say. This is like some cheesy TV movie."

"Here," he said, reaching into his pocket and handing her a set of keys.

"What are these?"

"Keys to a suite at the extended stay hotel on Davenport."

"An extended stay hotel? Seriously?"

"I've paid for six weeks after the house closes to give you some time to get on your feet."

Julie stood there in stunned silence. This wasn't the man she knew. This wasn't the man who nursed her back to health after a bout with the flu four years ago. This wasn't the man who diligently went to every Lamaze class with her when she was pregnant with Colleen. This certainly wasn't the man who stood in front of her and renewed his vows a few years back. She didn't know this guy.

"I just can't believe this."

"I need to also tell you the beach deal isn't happening, Julie."

"Obviously."

"I'm truly very sorry to kill your dream of living there."

"I thought it was *our* dream," she said, softly, unable to stop the tears from flowing.

"It was never my dream, Julie. You knew I was just going along."

"And what is your dream, Michael?"

"My dream is in Boston."

And just like that, her heart shattered into a million pieces, scattering all over the floor of a home that once housed only precious memories.

CHAPTER 2

The weeks that followed were a blur. Michael had left the next day, just like he said he would. He was gone before she woke up. Her night had been spent softly weeping in several parts of her home. First, it was their bedroom. She'd sat upright on her side of the bed, her knees pulled to her chest, rocking herself and sobbing as quietly as one could.

Meanwhile, Michael was sleeping in the upstairs guest room, probably texting his beloved - slightly younger - girlfriend. The thought made her sick to her stomach.

Then, she went to the bathroom and sat on the edge of the large garden tub. She thought about their last anniversary and how she'd wanted them to take a bath together with the jets on and a nice bottle of wine. But Michael had said he was tired and went to bed early. At the time, she took him at his word, but now she knew better. He'd felt guilty because his girlfriend had been pregnant at the time, sitting somewhere in Boston, wondering when he was coming home again.

Finally, she'd slipped out onto the deck and stared up at

the black night sky, which was slightly obscured by grayish white clouds, much like her life right now. She thought about how weird life was, that sometimes the last thing happens and you didn't know it was going to be the *last* thing.

Like her morning breakfasts on the deck with Michael. She hadn't known the one they had last week was the *last* one. He had. That was unnerving. How had she not seen the signs?

After he'd left - without a word or a look - the next morning, Julie had rattled around her now *very* empty house and thought about her next move. Much of the time, she jangled the keys to the extended stay hotel in the palm of her hand and thought about how her dream of living at the beach was vanishing before her very eyes. She'd never considered a life without Michael. Marriage was for keeps. It was forever. She'd thought he believed the same.

She also spent time looking on social media, spying on every Victoria in the Boston area. She looked for hours one night, buoyed by strong coffee and the occasional glass of wine. After looking at herself in the mirror, she realized that it was a bad road she was on and closed the computer.

And then the day came where Meg called from overseas, her voice shaky and her nose stuffed up. Julie prayed it was a cold, but she knew better.

"Daddy called me," was all she said before bursting into tears again.

"I'm so sorry, sweetie."

"How could he do this to us?"

"I don't know. I had no idea."

"I'm coming home."

"No, Meggy. You can't."

"Mom, you need at least one of us to come home. And Colleen has her big internship now. I can miss a semester and..."

"No! And that's final. Look, it's going to be hard, but I'll make it through. I promise."

"Are you sure? You've never been alone."

She wasn't sure at all. Not even a little bit. But she was a mother, and mothers have to fake being sure most of the time.

"I'm sure. I'm going to keep working, find myself a new place to live and get used to being a single woman. We'll get through this, Meg."

Meg sniffled. "I know. I love you."

"I love you too."

If the call with Meg had been hard, the one with Colleen had been almost impossible. At first, it went much the same, but Colleen was blunt and stubborn. She wasn't crying. She was livid, and Julie could practically hear the smoke shooting out of her ears from the other side of the country.

"I don't know what's gotten into Dad! Ya'll have always been the epitome of a perfect marriage."

"Nobody's marriage is perfect, Colleen."

"Well, I'm not talking to him. I don't want to see him. And I sure don't want to see his home wrecking fiancee!"

"Wait. Fiancee?"

Colleen was silent for a moment. "You didn't know?"

"No. I didn't." Julie's face felt like it was beet red as anger rose up once again. "We're not even divorced."

"That's what I said, but apparently the papers are almost ready. I guess you should prepare yourself."

"I know he's your father, so I'm not going to say what I want to say right now."

"Mom, I can come home. I'll get an internship near Atlanta, so at least I'll be closer to you instead of across the country."

"No. As I told your sister, I need this time to myself. I'll be fine. I just want to get the divorce over with, get settled in a new house and start making new memories."

"What about Aunt Janine? I'm sure she'd love to hear from you…"

"Colleen, enough. You know how broken my relationship is with my sister. I haven't spoken to her since you were in high school, and I don't plan to start now."

Just the mention of her older sister's name made Julie nauseous. The two of them had grown up pretty close, much like Meg and Colleen had. But as they got older, their personality differences seemed to grow as wide as the Grand Canyon. Janine, ever the world traveler and wanna-be flower child, didn't understand when Julie decided to settle down right out of college with Michael. She thought he was a stick in the mud, and maybe she was right. But, even now, Julie found herself wanting to defend his honor.

Finally, when the kids were in high school, she and Janine had had such a blowout that their relationship was irretrievably broken. Sometimes, family isn't just about blood. And the last thing she needed right now was her flighty, all too strange sister showing up and wrecking her life.

Her sister had tried, at times, to reach out to her over the years. There was a time when she was at a yoga training retreat in some part of Indonesia that Julie couldn't pronounce. She had received postcards and letters from just about every corner of the globe, always with Janine rambling on about the crazy paths that her life had taken her on. All the while, Julie was at home, being the good wife, mother and responsible citizen she had always been.

If she was being honest with herself, there might of been a little jealousy at play. Everyone liked Janine growing up. She was loud, fun loving and said all the things that people were thinking but afraid to say out loud. But she was also irresponsible and constantly on the move, making it difficult to rely on her as a sister.

She had missed so many Easters and Christmases and birthdays for the girls because she was too busy gallivanting all over the place. Not to mention all of the different men she went through. It was like she considered them to be recyclable.

Julie didn't understand her and never would. She decided she'd rather be alone than be involved with her sister again. It just wasn't worth the turmoil as she definitely had plenty of that in her life right now.

"Okay. I was just trying to help, Mom. I hate to see you lonely."

"Sweetie, there's a difference between being lonely and being alone. I don't think being alone is necessarily a bad thing."

Even as she said it, she knew it wasn't true. She still wanted her old memories. She wanted the husband she *thought* she had. She wanted to rewind and beg Michael to never go to Boston in the first place. She wanted a do-over.

As the days wore on, she went from feeling loss and pity for herself to feeling anger toward Michael and finally to feeling anger at herself for caring about him. She wanted to not care about him at all, to wipe his face from her memory.

But every moment in the house they shared together for all those years felt like an eternity now. She just wanted to get to the closing table, sign the papers and be done with it all.

"Mrs. Pike? Please come this way. The closing is in our conference room." The woman led her down the hallway, lined with thick mahogany furniture and overly ornate paintings. No one was in the room yet as Julie was always early. "Would you like some coffee or tea?"

"No thanks."

"Would you like to review the paperwork prior to the closing? I can bring the file…"

"No, thank you."

"Alright then. The other parties should be here shortly."

Julie nodded.

A large bowl of chocolate candy sat in the middle of the long, mahogany table. In her current stressed out state of mind, she thought about dumping as much of it into her purse as she could fit, but the attorney walked in before she could do it.

"Mrs. Pike?" he said, reaching out his hand.

"Yes, that's me," she said, rising from her chair slightly as she shook his hand. For a moment, she thought about her name. Mrs. She was about to be a Ms. Or could she go back to Miss? Maybe those days were over. What was the protocol? She'd never really thought about it.

"The buyer's are coming in just a moment. Would you like any coffee? I can get my secretary to…"

"No thank you. Just ready to get the papers signed as soon as poss…"

Julie looked up to see Michael walking into the room. He was alone, thank goodness. She had no interest in seeing his new fiancee.

"Hey," he said under his breath as he sat down beside her.

"Hello." She thought about how this would be the last time they signed anything together as a couple. Well, except divorce papers, but they wouldn't have to sit beside each other to do it.

"How are you?" he asked softly as the buyers made their way into the room and started chatting with the attorney.

"Please don't act as if you care, Michael."

"Of course I care, Jules… Julie, I mean."

She couldn't look at him. Here was the man she'd loved her whole life, yet the thought of sitting next to him made her sick. He'd not only been lying to her, but he'd been lying in the bed with another woman for almost two years. How hadn't she seen the signs?

"Okay, folks, I guess we can get started. This big stack of papers might look time consuming, but a lot of it is disclosures and so forth. We should be able to get through it all in about twenty minutes or so. Most of this is for the buyers, so let's begin on this side of the table…"

Julie stared off into space for most of the process, only perking up when the attorney turned to their side of the table. She felt so alone, so lonely, even though her husband was sitting there. The man whose hand she'd held for over twenty years was within reach, but also not within reach. Her heart was still attached to his, but his was already with someone else. It all felt so cold and strange and sad.

"Mrs. Pike, I wanted to ask you about the front flower bed. How did you keep it so manicured?" the woman across from her asked. She and her husband, obviously excited about their new home and totally in love, looked giddy as they signed the papers for their first home. Young and in love. She felt that way once. A long time ago. Now, she just felt rage and a few occasional homicidal feelings.

She wanted to grab the woman's hands and warn her that men changed. That she'd better be on guard and watch him because he could leave her in the lurch in an instant. She wanted to urge her to keep things in her name, and to always have a good attorney on speed dial. Romance, shmomance.

"Oh, I… we hired a service." She wrote down the name of the company and slid it across the table, doing her best to be cordial when she really just wanted to get out of there.

"I love the adorable archway you built in the back!"

"We renewed our vows there a few years ago," she said without thinking. Her eyes welled with tears as she remembered that day. Both of her girls served as honorary bridesmaids while their friends and family watched them renew their love at the fifteen year mark.

"Julie, you're my world. You always have been. There will never be a day that I don't love you. I promise to always put you first and to spend the rest of my life thanking God for you."

What had gone wrong since then?

"I bet we'll do the same one day, right, babe?" the woman said as she turned to her husband and gave him a quick kiss. Julie wanted to flee the scene. Babe. She'd always hated that term of endearment. Today, especially.

"Maybe we should get back to signing the papers," Michael said, sensing Julie's discomfort. Was he trying to protect her? Probably not. More than likely, he was trying to get back to his hussy and love child.

"Okay, here's the closing statement. If everyone can take a look at their side, we'll start here at the top…"

For the next few minutes, they stared at a long, legal sheet of paper with more numbers than Julie had ever seen. Normally, Michael handled this type of thing. Numbers were never her forte. She was a brilliant writer, decorator and cook, but numbers made her eyes cross.

Julie looked at the last number which was their profit on the sale. Of course, it would be split down the middle when they each walked away. Twenty-one years of marriage would be done soon, and she'd get her cut of the money to start over as a single woman. Never had she thought she would have that title again.

Although her online business had given them some fun money over the years, it likely wouldn't support her once the house money ran out. No matter what, she'd have to get a job, and that thought terrified her. She hadn't worked since before Colleen was born, and she'd never intended to go back. Who'd want to hire a forty-three year old woman who hadn't worked in over twenty years?

Sure, she could ask for alimony in the divorce, but there was a large part of her that was too prideful to do it. She didn't want a long fight in court, and she didn't want his tainted money flowing into her bank account each month. It didn't make logical sense, but it was the way she felt.

She felt pretty sure Michael was hiding money somewhere that he was using to support his skank and kid. Thinking of ways to describe the woman was her new hobby, although it probably wasn't the right thing to do.

As they wrapped up the closing, the buyers hugged her without warning. She tried to be nice, but she just wanted to get to her car as quickly as possible without talking to Michael again. Any future communication would be through their attorneys.

The paralegal handed her a check which was her half of the money from the sale. Julie slipped it into her purse and walked quickly out of the office into the parking lot. As if life hadn't been hard enough in the last couple of weeks, she was met by a woman who was holding an adorable little boy. The woman's eyes popped open as she tried to turn back toward her car.

"Victoria, I thought you were waiting in the car..." Michael said from behind.

"I'm sorry, honey. Charlie had a little accident, so I was trying to make it to the bathroom."

Julie stared at her, unable to move her legs. She was gorgeous, and she sure as heck didn't look just a year younger. Her picture was probably next to "voluptuous" in the dictionary, and her hair was black as midnight and hung almost to her waist. The little boy was adorable and would probably grow up to be a model himself.

"You're Victoria." That was all she could say. No other words were coming out.

"Yes," she said quietly. Michael reached over and took the

boy, standing back a bit as if he wasn't sure what was about to go down. Julie continued staring at her. "I'm not sure what to say."

"You knew he was married?"

Victoria looked at Michael and then back at Julie. "Not at first. But yes, for most of the time we've..."

"Been sleeping together," Julie said, finishing her sentence.

"Okay." Why didn't this woman seem apologetic?

Julie took in a deep breath, determined to take the high road. "Just remember this. What they'll do *with* you, they'll do *to* you. Good luck because you're going to need it."

Without looking back, Julie walked to her car. She cranked it, drove out of sight into another office park, turned it off and sobbed for half an hour before driving home to meet the movers.

CHAPTER 3

*J*ulie sat in her car, outside of the little bistro, and procrastinated. Why had she agreed to this? All she really wanted to do was get back to her extended stay suite, pop some macaroni and cheese into the mini microwave and watch a marathon of court TV shows. Maybe that would prepare her for the divorce proceedings that were coming up soon.

Instead, she'd stupidly agreed to lunch with her well-to-do friends from the country club. Mallory, Tiffany and Heidi were well meaning, most of the time. But they were just about as stuck-up and stereotypical rich housewives as any of the women she'd seen on reality TV. And they were literally carbon copies of each other, complete with seemingly perfect husbands and children.

Truth be told, she'd fallen into that stereotype herself a few times, but she'd always tried to come back to who she really was at her core. She was the daughter of Richard, an accountant, who had passed away when she was a junior in high school, and SuAnn, a stay-at-home mom for her and her sister's entire upbringing. SuAnn had never worked outside

RACHEL HANNA

of the home, didn't have a degree and was content baking and sewing and ringing the dinner bell that hung on their front porch every night when the street lights came on.

They'd lived a perfectly middle class life in their one-story brick ranch house on the outskirts of Atlanta. There'd been no country clubs or housekeepers or vacations when she was a kid. There were lots of homemade biscuits, pops on the legs with switches when they misbehaved and early morning Sunday school classes.

But her friends, as she loosely thought of them, hadn't experienced the same upbringing. They were all "from money", and marrying wealthy men had only intensified their status.

Mallory's father had invented something that had to do with cell phones back in the day, and her family had been rolling in dough ever since. When she married Devin, a software developer with a genius IQ, her life was set. They had three kids together, all of whom had white blond hair and looked like they belonged on a beach vacation brochure.

Tiffany had been raised with a silver spoon in her mouth too, but Julie had no idea where the money came from. Tiff didn't talk about it too much, and Julie had often wondered if there was some criminal activity in her family's past. Either way, when Tiff met Allesandro ten years ago, she was set for life too. The man was a freaking Italian race car driver and looked like he'd been chiseled from stone.

And then there was Heidi. She was a nice woman, but her level of intellect was right about the same as the Basset Hound Julie had loved growing up. Heidi just didn't drool... that she knew of, anyway. Heidi's mother had been a fashion designer back in France, where she was born, and Heidi had spent her early years on the runway. Her parents had moved to the US when Heidi was in high school, and she'd met Pierre, a French exchange student in the US at the time, and sparks flew. Their marriage was probably the most normal looking from the outside, but Pierre also traveled a lot like Michael, and that made Julie wonder.

"Are you coming or what?" Mallory asked, knocking on her window. She'd been so lost in thought that she hadn't noticed her friends looking at her from a table outside.

Julie forced a smile and opened her door. "Sorry. I was off in la la land for a minute."

Mallory poked out her lower lip and glanced at the table where Tiffany and Heidi sat, also with sad looks on their faces.

"I know, sweetie. We all heard what happened with Michael. Terrible! Just terrible! Come with me. We already have a bottle of wine and big basket of bread," she said, sliding her arm around Julie's waist like she was going to have to hold her up.

"Wine? It's not even noon yet..."

"Desperate times call for desperate measures!" Mallory said breathlessly as she ushered Julie to the table.

"I'm not really desperate, Mal..." she tried to say as they approached Heidi and Tiffany. Both women stood up and hugged her from opposite sides, Heidi taking the added measure to nuzzle her head against Julie's neck. The whole thing was a little much, and Julie noticed people staring.

"Can we just sit?" she whispered as she fake smiled at the people around them. When they all took their seats, Julie noticed the women staring at her with all the pity one would have looking at a matted, homeless dog on one of those late night TV commercials that are designed to make you sad and depressed right before going to sleep.

"Oh, Jules, we're all just so sorry about what's happened to you!" Heidi said, her lower lip poking out far enough to hold a large bird. Of course, her lips... and most of the rest of her body... were fake and plumper than God intended.

"Guys, I'm okay. Really. Please don't make a big deal out of this."

Tiffany cocked her head. "Fine? Darling, we know you're not fine. We heard what happened after the closing."

Julie stilled in her seat. "What do you mean?"

"It was all the talk at the club the next day. How you and the mistress had a loud argument right there in front of Michael's love child. I just can't imagine how you felt!"

"Tiff, there was no argument. None. We didn't even raise our voices."

"Well, either way, you must know that we're here to support you. We're on your side."

"There aren't going to be sides. Our attorneys are finalizing the paperwork, and soon this will all be over."

"Over?" Mallory said. "Sugar, this will never be over. You have kids with this man. He'll be bringing that tart to every family function, along with their child. Your daughters' weddings... when grandkids are born... and then their birthdays... You have a lifetime of him throwing this in your face. Surely, you must be devastated?"

It sounded like they wanted her to be devastated. And she was. In fact, she was completely shattered and spent most nights lying in her tiny hotel room bathtub with a pint of ice cream. But they didn't need to know that. Her mother, a problem in her life in her own right, had at least taught her to not let people see her sweat.

"Listen, the shock has worn off. Life goes on. I'm doing well, considering. I'd really rather not talk about this anymore. Can't we just have lunch like we've always done?"

"Oh. I guess we can try that," Tiffany said, scanning the other women's faces for agreement. They reluctantly nodded.

"Good. Now, what's the special today?" Julie asked,

looking at the menu she had memorized after going to the bistro dozens of times.

"The club sandwich, I believe," Mallory said.

"I'm sorry, but I have to ask," Heidi popped up, her way too perky French voice grating on Julie's nerves so early in the day.

"What?"

"Didn't you... notice?"

"Notice what, Heidi?" Julie asked, trying to give her a tone that would indicate her unwillingness to talk about this issue anymore. But Heidi was a ditz, and she didn't pick up on such social cues.

"Well, I mean, he was sleeping with this woman, right?"

Julie saw Mallory roll her eyes. "That's the requirement to have a love child."

Heidi giggled. "Oh, right. But, I mean, couldn't you tell he wasn't... that into *you*?"

"Heidi!" Tiffany scolded.

"Sorry. I just think my Pierre would show signs. You know, like not wanting to..." she said, not finishing her thought.

"Jules, you don't have to answer that," Mallory said.

"I'll just say this, Heidi. Michael showed no signs at home, but remember he was traveling a lot. Hmmm, come to think of it, a lot like your Pierre, right?"

Heidi stared at her for a long moment, her big brown eyes eventually popping open. "I need to make a call!" She grabbed her cell phone and ran toward the bathroom, and it was all Julie could do not to laugh.

"Seriously, how are you?" Mallory asked, a genuine look of concern in her eyes.

Julie paused. These were the only friends she had right now, even if they weren't exactly the best ones she could imagine. Maybe she shouldn't write them off so quickly. After all, who else did she have right now that she could count on? Her daughters were far away, Michael was gone, her mother was too much to take at the moment, and her sister - yeah, that would be a big, fat no thank you. Family drama on top of losing her marriage wasn't on her list of things to pursue. It was one of the reasons she hadn't told her mother about the pending divorce. She didn't need any of her backhanded remarks not-so-cleverly disguised as "helpful advice".

"It's tough right now."

Tiffany reached across and touched her hand. "I'm sorry, honey. I really am."

"Where are you staying?" Mallory asked as Heidi reappeared at the table, eyes red.

"At the extended stay place down the road."

"Extended stay? What does that mean?" Heidi asked, wiping her eyes with a cloth napkin.

"It means my cheating ex thought he was doing me a favor by getting me a studio suite at a cheap hotel for a few weeks."

"And then what?" Mallory asked.

"I don't really know. I haven't made any definitive plans."

"You are welcome to stay with me and Allesandro. We have that whole in-law suite available, you know," Tiffany offered. Julie smiled, gratefully.

"I appreciate it, Tiff, but I need to start over. On my own. I don't even know where I'll end up."

"Wait. You're not staying here?" Heidi asked.

"I'm not sure. I'm weighing all of my options."

"But you can't leave, Jules. You're on the board at the club. And the tennis team needs you!" Heidi said, her voice traveling higher and higher.

Julie literally bit her tongue. Her entire life had fallen

apart, and all one of her closest "friends" could think about was the club and the tennis team?

"I resigned from the board yesterday. And the team will be fine without me."

Tiffany poked her lip out again. "Listen, you don't have to give up your whole life, Julie."

"What do you mean?"

Tiffany leaned toward her and the other women followed suit. "I know a matchmaker in Atlanta. She has the wealthiest single men in the Southeast on speed dial. A quick trip to the salon to update your hairstyle…"

"Stop!" Julie heard herself saying way too loudly. People at tables around them turned to look. The women all sat back, their eyes wide and Heidi's mouth hanging open. "I've tried to be nice here, but back off! My whole life has fallen down around me, and all ya'll can talk about are tennis teams, boards and matchmakers. I don't want another man right now, and maybe ever. My nerves are raw. My heart is broken. All of this surface level crap is way down my list of things to worry about!"

"Sorry," Tiffany said, but in a sarcastic way. She crossed her arms and didn't make eye contact.

"Forgive me for saying so, sweetie, but this attitude isn't going to inspire people to help you out of this mess," Mallory said, taking a long drink of her wine.

"Help me out of what mess?"

The table was quiet for a moment before Tiffany finally spoke again. "Look, we're trying to help you save some face here. Michael's actions have tarnished your family name all over town. He's in Boston now, but you're here. If you want to stay in your current social circle…"

Now, Julie's mouth dropped open. "Seriously? You think I care about my social standing right now?"

"Darling, you should. At this point, you can still salvage

everything you've built here. But if you keep melting down in parking lots... and at bistros," she whispered. "Well, let's just say there's only so much we can do for you."

Suddenly, Julie felt like a stranger in a strange land. Who were these people? Were these the same women she'd spent so much time with on couples' trips and at charity events? The ones she thought were good people, albeit a bit vapid?

They were much, much worse. In that moment, she realized she couldn't stay in this town anymore, but not because of her reputation. It was because she didn't want to be thought of like she was currently thinking of these women.

"I have to go," Julie said, her own voice incredulous.

"Go? But we haven't had lunch yet," Heidi said, holding up her menu as if Julie didn't understand how to order lunch or something.

Julie stood and looked at each woman's face, all made up with expensive cosmetics and touched up by Dr. Kauffman, the local plastic surgeon. They were shells of real people, only seeking to get the approval of people who didn't really care about them. Had she been doing the same thing all these years? Trying to get the approval of these women? People at the country club? And for what? What had it all meant? The big house, the maid - even though she adored her - the expensive cars?

She was alone. Her marriage had been a facade, apparently. Her kids were wonderful, despite it all, but even they were gone. Her only chance at having a life was getting away from this place and these people.

Julie turned and walked toward her car without saying a word, Mallory and Tiffany hot on her heels. "Where are you going?"

She turned to them and smiled for the first time in weeks. "I'm going to live my dream, that's where I'm going."

She climbed into her car, turned the key and contemplated what her dream really was.

~

JULIE COULDN'T BELIEVE what she was doing. Who in the world would spend their nest egg on a fixer upper beach house in a town they'd never visited without ever visiting the house in person?

Her. That's who would do such a thing.

She had obviously lost her mind.

Meg was worried about her and threatening to fly home almost daily. Only, home wasn't their home anymore.

Colleen had taken to giving her nightly talks that involved therapy terminology she was apparently reading on the Internet.

But it felt right for some reason. Even though she'd gone about it all wrong.

Now, there was no turning back. She was driving over the bridge onto Seagrove, a small island off the coast of South Carolina that was barely a dot on the map. During her online pursuit of property, Seagrove Island had come up a couple of times in her price range, but most people had never even heard of it.

A part of her was dubious, of course. She'd always been a practical kind of person who needed everything in the right place and a super clean house. That hadn't bothered her sister, who she shared a bedroom with for most of her life. No, Janine had been what Julie would later call a "beginner hoarder", keeping every movie stub, gum wrappers with jokes on them and every note her best friend in seventh grade had passed to her in class.

But Julie hadn't been that way at all. She wanted order, in her life and in her space. So, jumping into a fixer upper with no experience even hanging her own pictures on the wall was daunting to say the least.

As she drove over the bridge onto Seagrove, she was astonished at just how small it was. The tallest building she saw was two stories, and houses were few and far between. Her little bit of research on the town had only yielded bits of info about its history and important historical buildings. But she didn't know much about living there because only about one-hundred people called it home. One-hundred. Could they even call it a town with that few people?

She glanced around at the little mom and pop shops that littered the area, looking for somewhere she could get a job when she was ready. There was a place called "The Shrimp Shack", but that didn't seem like the career path she wanted to take. Getting a job might prove harder than she anticipated. Luckily, she'd gotten a great deal on her house, but the repairs would need to be done out of the money she had left, which wasn't all that much.

Her online boutique was struggling, as it usually did during the summer months, but at least it had paid for the movers to bring her things in a week or so. For now, she only had what was in her small car, and that was enough for her.

Looking at her GPS, Julie turned down the street the house was on. It was covered in a canopy of trees, thick moss hanging from them that made it almost seem like nighttime, only intricate streams of sunlight on the street, like little pieces of artwork.

She felt her palms sweating from nervousness. What if she pulled up and the house was unlivable? What if it was overrun with alligators or some other terrifying creature?

"Your destination is on the right in one hundred feet," the pleasant sounding woman on her GPS said. She was almost afraid to look.

She stopped her car in front of the short driveway and

took in a deep breath before finally turning to look at her new home. It wasn't as bad as she had feared it would be. In fact, it was quite cute with the same moss covered trees dotting the front yard and the little white cottage standing out like an angel in the midst of the shade.

The island was only about three miles long in total, with the width only about half a mile in most places. It was surrounded by water; on one side, the Atlantic Ocean and on the other side filled with tidal creeks and marshes. Her little cottage sat on the marshland, which wasn't exactly what she'd wanted at the beginning, but the ocean was only down the dirt road a bit.

She had no neighbors around as the cottage was at the tip of the island in a mostly uninhabited area. From what the real estate agent had told her, most people wanted to buy in the beach areas, and homes there rarely came up for sale. When they did, the price was more than double what she paid, even for a fixer upper.

Starting over required compromise, and if being so close to the ocean meant she had to swat mosquitos and look out for alligators every so often, she would gladly take one for the team. Well, for her team of one, anyway.

She got out of her car and walked up the short gravel driveway, looking around her lot as she did. It wasn't big, but it was hers. She was proud of her purchase so far. It was the first thing she'd ever really done for herself as an adult. After all, she'd gone from her parents' home to her dorm to her married home. There was never a moment she lived alone.

She walked up onto the small porch and immediately noticed the rotting wood with holes scattered around. That would be high on her list of things to fix as she had no intentions of falling through her own porch. No telling what was underneath it.

She turned the key, the sound of birds and bugs she'd

never heard before playing in the air. That would take some getting used to. The whole area was like something out of a book or a movie, with vegetation growing she'd never seen in person.

The door stuck as she pushed on it, age and battered chips of paint keeping it from opening. She leaned back and hit it three times with her shoulder before it finally opened, a plume of dust hitting her in the face like powder shooting from a fire extinguisher.

"Yuck!" she said to no one in particular. She rubbed the dust from her eyes and opened them to reveal a house in shambles. The outside had been deceiving. The place was a wreck with holes in the hardwood floors, dust and yellow pollen covering every surface and some smell she couldn't quite identify yet.

"Oh my gosh…" she said, holding out the last word as she looked from room to room, trying to find a place she could sleep safely. That would be impossible. The place needed a thorough cleaning before she could even think of sleeping there. Plus, there was no bed, no air conditioning and no electricity. How had she been so naive as to think she could stay there even for a night? Had she wasted all of her money on a death trap no one else had wanted?

In despair, she walked out onto the back porch, which had weirdly been renovated recently, and stared into the marsh. The sunset was beginning, and streaks of pink and orange swept across the sky like God had painted it himself. Unable to hold in her emotions, she began to weep.

She wept because this place wasn't even close to being habitable.

She wept because her marriage was over.

She wept because even in that shambles of a house, the sky made her believe anything was possible.

Possible, not probable. But what choice did she have?

CHAPTER 4

*J*ulie drove around the island and finally found a small inn at the other end. The place didn't look much bigger than her own, but it was in pristine condition and had a sign in the front from the local historical registry. Whoever owned it was meticulous in the way they cared for it. The cream colored boards were accented by navy blue trim and shutters, and the ocean sat in the background like a perfect picture postcard. It was a totally different scene than the one playing out on her lot.

"Lancaster House" was carved into the wooden sign that sat at the end of the road. The home was built in 1918 according to the sign, but it looked brand new.

There was an "open" sign in the window and a couple of lights on in the front room, an orange glow the only illumination other than the quickly setting sun. Julie stepped out of her car, slung her bag over her back and prayed to God the place had a vacancy as she walked up the three steps to the front door.

The bugs of the marsh nearby seemed to be preparing a full choral concert as they got louder and louder. It occurred to her that this would take some getting used to, all of the noises and colors and smells.

She heard the door open and looked up to see a man, maybe a little younger than her, standing there. He had what her grandmother would've called a "lazy smile" with one side of his mouth turning up more than the other. He leaned against the open front door, one arm above his head touching the top of the frame. He wore a pair of khaki shorts, a baby blue t-shirt and no shoes.

"Can I help you?" he asked, his Southern drawl deeper and more authentic than any accent she'd heard before. It sounded like he'd stepped right out of Gone With The Wind, one of her favorite movies of all time. She would still marry Rhett Butler right on the spot if he appeared in front of her - and wasn't a completely fictional character.

"Yes. I'm Julie. I bought the cottage at the other end of the island."

"Oh, yes, the cottage on the cove, right?"

Cottage on the cove. It had a nice ring to it. She wanted to say she bought the deathtrap on the dirt road, but that didn't sound nearly as fancy.

"Right."

He smiled and looked at her. "Was there more to that story?"

She was so tired. And hot. And sticky. Why was it so dang sticky here?

"I'm sorry. It's been a very long day. I'm looking for a place to stay for the night."

"You can't stay at your house?"

She shook her head. "It's a little less... habitable... than I imagined."

He chuckled. "You mean you didn't come see it in person before you bought it?"

She hung her head. "No, I didn't. I had to move kind of…quickly. I took a chance."

"Ah. Well, should I worry that you're some kind of fugitive? Having to leave quickly and all that."

Gosh, his voice sure was nice. She felt like she needed to lay down in a hammock and sip a mint julep right about now.

"No. Not a fugitive. So, do you have a vacancy?"

"Sure. Come on in," he said, opening the door further and waving for her to come in. "Here, let me take your bag."

Without waiting for a response, he took it from her shoulder and shut the door behind them. It occurred to her that she was now alone in a house on a sparsely inhabited island with a strange man who was better looking than any real live human she'd ever seen. This was one of those murder shows she watched and shook her head at.

"Why was the woman dumb enough to believe that guy and get in his car?"

"Who would be stupid enough to go into a house alone with a strange man?"

Yep, she was now the dumb woman she always wondered about.

"Lucy?" he called out. Before Julie could ask who that was, a woman appeared. She was wearing a simple floral house dress and looked like she'd stepped right out of Hawaii, but here she was in South Carolina.

"Yes?"

"We have an unexpected guest. Can you show her to the Savannah suite?"

He had suites? The house didn't seem big enough for that.

"Sure, hon," she said, her drawl as thick as his. "Follow me, sweetie," she said, as the man handed her Julie's bag. Lucy was a larger, curvy woman, probably her mother's age or maybe a bit more. Her skin was the color of Julie's favorite latte drink, and her eyes were as black as midnight. Julie wished her pale white skin - that her grandmother called "porcelain" - would even turn a shade darker to "off white", but the only color she ever turned was red. And then she peeled like some kind of weird lizard, and she was white all over again.

She followed Lucy up the narrow staircase and to a room down the hall. Everything was expertly decorated for the time period, and Julie found herself wishing she'd just bought this place instead of her dump down the street.

Maybe she just needed a good night's sleep. Perhaps everything would look, and feel, better in the morning. The only problem was that she wasn't really tired. She was exhausted mentally. Her muscles hurt. But she wasn't going to be able to actually sleep for a few hours. In fact, she realized she hadn't even had dinner yet.

"Hey, Lucy?" she called to the woman before she left the room.

"Yeah, hon?"

"I'm a bit hungry. Is there a restaurant on the island?" She hoped there was some place other than The Shrimp Shack. That place truly looked like a shack.

Lucy giggled. "There are a couple, but nobody's open at this hour."

Julie picked up her phone and looked at the time. It was just after eight-thirty.

"They don't stay open for dinner?"

"Sugar, dinner's at six around here. They're all closed up by this time of night. You ever lived on an island?"

Julie shook her head. "No, ma'am."

"Well, get used to a new way of life, hon. Island time is very different than regular time. We close up shop early and go home to enjoy the sounds of the marsh and the moonlit views of the ocean. We ain't about working on the island."

Julie smiled. "I kind of like that mentality."

"If you're hungry, I can make you a sandwich out of the roast beef we had for dinner."

"Oh, that sounds delicious."

"Come on downstairs when you're ready then. I'll get you all fixed up." Lucy shut the door behind her as Julie stood in the middle of the room and looked around.

It occurred to her that she was currently homeless. Yes, she'd bought a house, but what good was that if she couldn't live there? And she certainly couldn't afford to keep staying at the inn for weeks on end.

She had a lot to think about, and a lot of worries to stew over, but right now she needed food in her belly.

～

JULIE SAT at the dining table in the dimly lit room. The table was heavy and looked recently handmade, but matched the time period. The original wallpaper covered the walls, and the thick moulding lined the room around the ceiling. Although the house was small, the ceilings were high and made everything look bigger.

An antique vase sat in the middle of the table full of some kind of brightly colored local flower she couldn't yet identify. Vintage dishes, some with cracks and chips, sat in a corner cabinet lit with little bulbs to show off the contents. It was very homey for someone with no home.

"Here ya go, hon," Lucy said as she sat the plate in front of her.

"Oh, wow. My grandmother had these same dishes," Julie said, taking a moment to smile and remember all the times she'd eaten her grandmother's famous homemade pound cake off of the very same plates.

Lucy smiled. "Memories are a good thing to have when we're a bit lost, aren't they?"

Julie nodded. "Do I look lost?"

"You sure do, like a fish outta water," she said with a chuckle.

"I guess I'm not a great actress."

"We all get lost once in awhile, but the island has a way of bringing us back to life."

"I hope that's the case with me."

Lucy turned and poured Julie a glass of sweet tea, setting it in front of her. "Give it time. Let the island do its work."

The way she spoke, with such authority and wisdom, made Julie miss her grandmother, who she had affectionately called Gigi.

Gigi had made her feel safe even in the worst of times. She missed her everyday even though she'd been gone for years.

"If there's nothing else right now, I think I'll go finish tidying up the kitchen," Lucy said, smiling.

"Please, don't let me stop you from doing your work. I'm very thankful for the sandwich, though. Please put it on my tab."

Lucy chuckled and shook her head. "You really don't get how island life works, do ya?" She continued laughing as she pushed open the swinging door to the kitchen.

Maybe Julie didn't get island life just yet.

"How's the sandwich?" she heard a voice say from behind her. It was the man again. This time, he was leaning against the doorframe on the other side of the room. What was it with this guy and leaning?

"Amazing. Thank you so much. I told Lucy to put it on my tab."

He chuckled just like Lucy had.

"What's so funny?"

The man walked around and sat down at the other end of the table. In the dim light, with only the orange glow of a couple of oil lamps and a candle in the middle of the table, he looked like some kind of hero from a romance novel come to life. He had brown hair, a bit long, almost to his shoulders. Michael had never let his hair grow past his ears, which always made him look a little bit too put together and more on the nerdy side.

Even though the man's hair was brown, there were streaks of yellow throughout as if he'd been bathing in the sun every day of his life. And then there was the tan, a golden brown that rivaled anything she'd seen on all of those suntan oil bottles at the drug store.

"On Seagrove, we're big on hospitality. Sandwiches are free, especially for new guests to our little oasis."

"Really? Well, thank you. I don't know what I would've done if I hadn't found this place. Can you tell me the daily rent? I'll be glad to put my credit card on file…"

"Oh, we don't take credit cards."

"Just cash?"

He smiled, that one side of his mouth rising up higher than the other. "What's your name again?"

"Julie."

"Well, Julie, I'm Dawson Lancaster," he said, reaching across the table and shaking her hand. His hands were so large, much like he was. She wouldn't have taken him for an innkeeper if she'd seen him out in public. More like a lumberjack with his height and muscular build.

"Oh, as in Lancaster Inn? How long have you owned this place?"

"It's been in my family for generations. I've lived here since I was a kid. The island is in my blood, I guess you could say."

"Do you get a lot of visitors?"

"Here? Nah. Not really. Just the occasional tourist who ventures out this way to look for gators."

"Maybe you could do more marketing? I'm sure people would love to stay here if they knew what a beautiful place this was." He smiled again. It was like he and Lucy were keeping a secret. "Okay, what's so funny?"

She was starting to feel uncomfortable and a little perturbed. Plus, she was hot, sticky and tired, so she really just wanted to get upstairs to take a cool bath in the clawfoot tub she saw.

"Well, Miss Julie, I hate to tell ya this, but the inn hasn't been in operation since the eighties when my grandma still ran it and I lived in the attic."

She stared at him for a long moment. "I don't understand. There's an open sign right over there in the window."

"We keep it on in honor of Granny. She never met a stranger and sure as heck wouldn't turn anyone away."

"Why didn't you just tell me you weren't open to guests?" Now, she was really embarrassed. She'd basically interrupted this poor guy's life and invited herself to stay at his house for the night. Or longer.

"My Granny would haunt me for the rest of my days if I'd turned you away, especially being a new neighbor and all."

"I'm so sorry about all of this," she said, starting to stand up. "I'll just drive over to the mainland and check into a hotel over there…"

He stood up. "No, don't do that. We enjoy the company. I only told you because you seemed intent on giving me money, and I don't want your money."

Julie slowly sat back down, glad she didn't have to leave, at least for the night. "Okay, but I promise I'll be out of your hair first thing in the morning."

"I don't think that's going to work."

"Why is that?"

"The rally starts tomorrow on the mainland. All the hotels are booked solid for the next week."

"Rally?"

"Motorcycles. Happens every year. It's crazy over there. Even if there was a room, I sure wouldn't recommend a lady stay over there by herself during the rally."

She didn't know whether to be offended that he thought she couldn't take care of herself or feel protected by this total stranger.

"This whole thing is a disaster," she moaned, putting her head in her hands and almost into her sandwich.

"The cottage, you mean?"

"I can't believe what a mistake I made. And I can't afford... I don't know why I'm telling you all of this. I'm a terrible house guest."

He smiled. "I don't get much company on this end of the island. I could use a little conversation. So, tell me why you bought the house sight unseen."

She sighed. "I'm in the middle of a divorce that I wasn't expecting. We sold the home we'd owned together for all those years, and I used my half to buy that place. It wasn't much, and I guess now I know why. It's just that I have always dreamed of living at the beach."

Dawson smiled. "This place will draw you in. The cottage just needs a little sprucing up."

She rolled her eyes. "I think you're putting it mildly. I almost had a mental breakdown when I went inside."

He chuckled. "Ah, I've seen worse. Just needs a little elbow grease and imagination."

"Do you know any contractors I can call? I mean, I can do a lot of the clean up work myself, but there are some projects I'll need to get quotes on."

"Sure. I've got a business card around here somewhere. I'll be sure to leave it on the front table when I find it."

"Okay. Thanks. I really do appreciate your hospitality, Dawson. I feel a bit out of my element here."

"Don't you worry, Julie. The island never lets anyone go. You'll get the hang of it, and then you'll never want to be anywhere else."

"I sure hope you're right."

CHAPTER 5

*a*s Julie drove back up to her new home, her stomach churned. What had she done? What would her friends back home think? Where was home now?

In reality, she didn't have any friends she could count on, and her home was no longer her home. Seagrove was her new home, but it felt more like the second biggest disaster of her life, with Michael taking that coveted number one spot.

She'd gotten up early and snuck out of the inn, leaving a note thanking Dawson. He'd also left her a business card on the front table for Seagrove Contracting, so she decided she'd call them and at least two others to get estimates for the work that needed to be done.

After leaving the inn, she'd driven back across to the mainland and found the nearest big box hardware store. She had to pick up whatever she needed to survive in her new home until it could be made livable. Her small car was now filled with an inflatable mattress, linens, a couple of battery powered fans, a small grill and battery operated lanterns. She was literally camping in her own home.

There were moments that rage crawled up out of her depths when she thought about why she was in this position in the first place. Michael. His inability to remain faithful in their marriage. And now he was living the comfortable life in Boston, his new fiancee and their precious baby boy by his side. Meanwhile, she was living in a swamp and about to camp out in her own living room. Good times.

She'd texted both of her girls, telling them about her new home. Of course, she'd downplayed it quite a bit. Colleen wasn't buying it and had questioned her like a prosecutor.

"I'm coming to help you," she'd said.

"No. I don't need help, sweetie. I'm a grown woman, and I can hire some help to get it in shape. I'll be fine."

Even as she'd typed it, she knew she was in for an uphill battle. But the last thing she wanted was for her girls to stop their lives to help her. Plus, if she was going to have the mental breakdown of her life, she'd rather do it alone.

Julie spent the day cleaning the place from top to bottom, at least trying to rid it of the dust and bugs that currently inhabited it. She scrubbed walls, mopped floors and poured bleach on any surface that could withstand it.

There were moments she questioned her sanity. Why wasn't she just leaving? Surely she could sell this place to someone else. Someone handier. Someone crazier. Some other sucker.

"I reckon this is going to require at least six months of work, ma'am."

"What? Six months?" she said, staring at the contractor in her living room. He was about as round as he was tall, and he smelled like an Italian restaurant. She wondered if it would take six months simply because he didn't have the stamina to finish it sooner.

"We're going to have to fix these holes in the floor, repair the walls, rebuild that porch…" As he started to list all of the things he was going to do, she zoned out. There was no way she was going to allow someone in her house for six months.

"Thanks for coming by, but I don't think this is a good fit." She walked him to the door and opened it.

"Alright then, but good luck. This place is a pit," the man said, grumbling as he passed her and waddled to his truck.

"Yeah, well tell me something I don't know!" she yelled as she slammed the door.

Once he was out of sight, she let out a scream that probably scared the heron that hung out behind her crappy little oasis.

"Yikes, you okay?" a voice said from behind her. She turned to see Dawson standing at the front door.

Julie sighed. "Oh, sorry. I didn't see you there. Do you know a real estate agent?"

"Of course. Why?"

"I think I need to sell this place and recoup some of my investment." She slid to the floor and leaned her head against the wall.

Dawson chuckled. "Not a good day so far?"

"I've met two contractors today, and both were way too high for my budget and quoted me months of work. I'm meeting one more, and if he concurs, I'm selling this place and running away from home."

He walked around the room, looking as he went. "This place does need a lot of work, but it has good bones. I remember when the Gilbert's owned it. They were this sweet little old couple. Never had any kids. I cut their small patch of grass when I was in middle school."

"Why did they move?"

"Mrs. Gilbert got Alzheimer's, so they moved closer to a niece in Orlando. As I understand it, they both ended up in the nursing home together. I imagine they're long since gone from this world," he said, staring at the mantel for a moment before turning back to her.

Julie worked her way back up to a standing position, hard as it was from all the hours of scrubbing. "I think I got in over my head here. I don't know the first thing about rehabbing a house, especially one like this."

"Oh, it's not so hard, honestly. We've had to renovate parts of the inn throughout the years, and it just takes a little extra thought because of the historical nature of these homes. But they're worth preserving."

Julie smiled sadly. "I'm sure you're right, but I'm lost here, Dawson. I don't know the sounds or the smells of the marsh. I don't recognize the birds. I don't know how to survive in a place like this." She was struggling to hold back tears as she realized how lonely she already felt.

Dawson walked over and put his hands on her shoulders, a feeling that felt unexpectedly welcome and familiar. She remembered when Michael would do that, usually in times of crisis like this. It had always made her feel safe and secure, but now he was doing that to someone else and she was reveling in the touch of a stranger in the middle of the woods.

"I'll help you."

She chuckled. "Thanks. I really do appreciate the offer, but I can't inconvenience you too. This job is just too big."

Dawson stepped back, cleared his throat and stuck out his hand. "Hi. I'm Dawson Lancaster."

Julie stared at him. "Yeah, I know…"

"I own Seagrove Contracting. We have a two o'clock appointment. Sorry I'm a little early."

"Wait. What?"

Dawson smiled. "The card I gave you was mine. I hope that was okay?"

"Yes, of course it was. And I appreciate you coming over here, but please don't feel obligated..."

"Julie?"

"Yes?"

"Can I at least look around and give you my estimate before you try to say no?"

She laughed. "Yes. Sorry. Why don't we start in the kitchen?"

For the next half hour, she walked him around the inside and outside of the house, pointing out every flaw and sighing so much she felt light headed. When they finished, they took a seat on the back porch on the old cast iron bench and stared at the marshland.

"So, here's my estimate," he said, handing her a piece of paper he'd been writing on the whole time they walked. "And I figure we'll need about three months."

She stared at the paper, her eyes wide. "Dawson, this is half of what the other contractors quoted me. I can't let you take such a hit on this job."

He smiled. "Then those guys were crooks. This is a fair bid, and I hope you'll consider it."

"Consider it? Are you kidding me? I'm struggling not to stand up and do a little dance right now!"

"I don't have great rhythm, but let's do it!" he said, standing up and doing some disco moves.

"Yikes, don't do that," she said, laughing. She stood and looked up at him. "Seriously, thank you. I was really thinking of walking away. But now I have a little hope that this place could really be something."

"Like a new beginning?"

"Yeah. I suppose so."

"Well, I like you, Julie, and I think you'd be a great addition to our little island. So, welcome home."

She looked out at the marsh again, and suddenly it didn't

look so bad. Maybe she could get used to this new life after all.

~

SLEEPING in a house that should have probably been condemned years ago wasn't easy, Julie decided, as she crawled out of her tent and back into her personal money pit. She wasn't feeling quite as worried and tormented this morning as she had been yesterday. Dawson seemed so sure of himself and his ability to turn the place into an actual home. She was thankful to have found a friend like him. Otherwise, the loneliness would be overwhelming.

She shuffled to the kitchen counter, her fuzzy slippers catching occasionally on the jagged parts of her hardwood floors. If she had gone barefoot for even a moment, she'd have been covered in splinters. It seemed every part of her new home needed TLC. Dawson was definitely going to earn every cent she paid him.

As she opened the cooler to retrieve the bottle of iced coffee she'd purchased in town the day before, she heard a knock at the front door.

"I didn't think you'd be here so early..." she said as she swung open the door, expecting to see Dawson there. Instead, her stomach knotted up as she stared into a face she wasn't expecting to see. "Mom?"

SuAnn, the biggest neat freak she'd ever known, looked around Julie into the house, her mouth agape. "Oh my goodness... what in the world?" She didn't even look at her daughter. Instead, she pulled her perfectly manicured hand up to her face and covered her mouth like she'd just seen the preacher shacking up with a local prostitute or something.

"What are you doing here, Mom? How'd you even know..."

"Colleen called me. And it's a good thing she did! You're homeless? Oh my goodness, what would your father think? Thank God he's dead because this would kill him!"

"Okay, that didn't really make any sense. And I'm not homeless, Mother. I bought this house, and I'm renovating it."

SuAnn chuckled. "Honey, you don't know the first thing about renovating a house."

"She doesn't, but I do," Dawson said from behind her.

Startled, Julie turned around. Was everybody trying to scare the crap out of her this morning? "Dawson, how'd you get in here?"

"I came through the back. I saw you had company and didn't want to interrupt."

"But I locked the door?"

He laughed. "The lock's broken. I'll fix that first."

She smiled, the same kind of smile someone gives when a kidnapper is holding them hostage and they're trying to give a signal.

"I'll start in the kitchen if that's okay?" he said. Julie nodded.

She turned back to her mother. SuAnn shook her head. "Julie, isn't it a little soon to be..."

"To be what?"

"Shacking up with a n'er do well? I mean, I know Michael jilted you, but who is this man? A plumber or something?"

Julie stepped out onto the porch and shut the door behind her. "Mother! Honestly! He's my contractor. Renovations start today. I'm sorry Colleen called you... believe me, we'll be having a conversation about that... but I'm fine. And I really don't have time to entertain a guest right now."

SuAnn put her hand on her heart. "Good Lord, I wouldn't want to stay here anyway. I'm staying over at the Cambridge

House. It's a lovely place, very historical. Pack your things and come with me. This is no place to live, sweetheart."

"This is my home."

SuAnn waved her hand like she was swatting a mosquito. "Oh, please, Julie. We both know you're just having a little mental breakdown. Now, I know it was hard when Michael left you, but you must confess there had to be a reason."

Julie seethed with rage inside. Her mother had always had a fondness for Michael, mostly because he made good money. In SuAnn's world, the man was supposed to bring in the money, and the woman was supposed to keep him happy no matter what. When Julie had started her boutique business, SuAnn had cautioned her not to let things slip at home.

"Let's not do this, Mother."

"You know I love you, dear. But I tried to tell you that, as a good wife, you needed to focus on your husband's needs."

"Well, my husband's needs were apparently between the legs of a woman in Boston."

"Julie Ann! Watch your mouth. My goodness, you're becoming like a swamp person."

"What does that even mean?"

"Just you never mind. Please, Julie, come back to the hotel with me. We can sort this out. We'll find you a nice place near me in the mountains."

"No, Mom. I'm not leaving here. I made a commitment to a new life and to this little island. It's my dream."

"My friend Cicely's daughter, Patricia, had a nervous breakdown last year after her husband ran off with that woman who played the ukulele down by the ice cream parlor. Anyway, the doctor gave her this medication that made her feel so much better. I can find out the name..."

"Stop! Dear God, why are you like this?"

"Like what?" SuAnn asked, her eyes wide. The sad part

was that her mother really didn't know that how she acted was perceived badly by other people. She just was who she was. Which was why Julie distanced herself as much as possible, only coming around on holidays and calling a couple of times a month to check in. It was the only way to save her sanity.

"Nothing. Listen, Mom, I appreciate that you drove all the way here to check on me. But I'm fine. I just needed some time to myself and a new beginning. Hopefully, you can understand that one day."

"Julie, I didn't just come here to check on you."

"What? Then why did you come here?"

"When Colleen called me, I could tell that she was really worried. I didn't want her to have to fly all the way back from California to check on you. She's doing great things, that one. I sure hope she finds a nice boy out there who will treat her well. But there was another reason why I came. Look, I'm getting older. And the one thing that I would want more than anything in this world is to have my whole family together at the holidays."

Oh. Julie knew what that meant. She was referring to the estranged relationship that Julie and Janine had with one another. She'd brought it up many times over the years, never understanding why Julie wouldn't come to Christmas if Janine was there. And most of the time that worked out because Janine traveled all over the place, never staying in any one spot very long.

"Mom, I know what you're getting at and nothing has changed. I'm going through a really difficult time in my life, and the last thing I need is more complications. I'm sorry, but the answer is no."

"Well, then, make room for Mommy," she said as she brushed past Julie and walked into the house. Julie turned around and watched her mother walk across the living room, her arms hugging her body like she was about to get the plague.

"Mom, what are you doing? "

"I'm staying here with you. I can't be sure that you're okay here by yourself on this little godforsaken island in this trash pit of a house, so I'm staying with you. I'm your mother, and I will take care of you."

Julie felt like she was going to throw up. How had this turned so abruptly? "Are you all right? You don't seem like yourself. And you just got finished telling me you didn't even want to come into the house, much less stay here."

"I don't. But you should know better than anyone, my dear sweet daughter, that I get what I want. I want my family together at the holidays, and I'm not leaving here until you agree."

"Mom, you're much more frustrating than normal today. Why are you bringing this up now? It's not even near the holidays?"

SuAnn looked around the room, her upper lip curling like she smelled something bad. "Because, if you and your sister are going to mend fences, you can't do it over the Christmas ham. You have to start now. You have to forge a relationship."

"I'm getting a really bad feeling about this."

SuAnn walked across the room, poked her head out the front door and waved her hand in the air.

"Mother, what are you doing?" Julie didn't feel like she had ever been this confused in her entire life, including the moment where her husband explained he had a baby with another woman.

"I'm doing what mothers always do. I'm taking charge and fixing a situation that needs to be repaired." She stood there, her chin upturned in defiance. The only problem was, Julie had no idea what the defiance was all about.

Before she could say another word, she saw the person she never thought she'd see standing at the bottom of her front steps. Her sister.

CHAPTER 6

The last person she had expected to see was her sister. Janine looked much the same, maybe a little thinner. Her once long, dark brown hair was lighter now, flecks of gray streaking through her thick mane. Julie had always been a bit jealous of her hair. Truth be told, she'd been jealous about a lot of things over the years, like Janine's bubbly personality, her ability to meet new people like it was a sport and her tiny little waist. It was tinier now, which didn't seem fair at all.

"Hey, sis," Janine said, finally making eye contact.

"Janine," Julie said back, her tone very expressive of how she felt right now. "Mom, what's going on here?"

"Julie, invite your sister in. Didn't I teach you anything about hospitality?"

Julie sighed and stepped back, opening the door for both of them. Her mother barged right back into the house with Janine behind her, barely looking up until she got inside. She looked around, although her facial expression didn't give anything away. And why was she carrying luggage... like she was staying?

"Is someone going to tell me what's going on?"

SuAnn jutted her chin out again. "I'm your mother, and I know what's best for you. You can't be out here alone, Julie. That's simply not an option."

"Mother, I'm forty-three years old. I can do what I want. And I'm not alone. I have my friend, Dawson, if I need anything."

"Honestly, darling, you're far too trusting," she said. She wasn't totally wrong. She'd trusted Michael, and where had that gotten her? "When the chips are down... and they're most assuredly down right now... the only people you can count on are family."

"My chips are just fine."

"I told you this wasn't a good idea," Janine suddenly said. Up until that time, she hadn't uttered a word. She had just stood there, shoulders down, eyes looking at the floor, what there was of it. It wasn't like her to be so low energy. She seemed beaten down, although Julie couldn't put her finger on just what was going on. A part of her was curious but the larger part of her really didn't want to know. She didn't want to get involved in this whole thing, whatever it was.

"For once, we agree on something," Julie said. She looked over at her mother. "I appreciate that you're concerned about me, but I'm fine. And even if I'm not fine, I will be. Yes, I've gone through a very difficult time recently, but this is my new beginning, and I'm actually starting to get excited about it."

"Julie, you've always been the type to just run into something without thinking. I think that's probably how we ended up in this position."

"We?"

"Family is family. And you girls have been separated for far too long. This is a great opportunity for you to spend some time together. Get to know each other again. You were so close when you were little."

Julie chuckled. "Mom, I think you're remembering things far differently than they actually were. Janine and I couldn't be more different, and that has only gotten worse as we've gotten older."

It was weird to talk about Janine as if she wasn't there, but it was like she wasn't. She was barely looking up. Just from a human standpoint, Julie was getting a little concerned.

"You two are sisters, and you need each other right now. And, I didn't want to tell you this…"

"Tell us what?" Julie asked.

SuAnn took in a deep breath and then turned toward one of the windows, looking out into the distance. "Dr. Archer gave me some unsettling news recently. I don't want to talk about it. I don't want it to become a big deal. But in a few months, it would really make me happy if both of my daughters were sitting across from each other at the Christmas dinner table, laughing and getting along." She turned and looked at her daughters. "I hate to use mom guilt, but it's all I have left."

"Mom, you didn't tell me anything was wrong. What did Dr. Archer say?" Janine asked, a look of worry on her face.

"Yes, Mom, you have to tell us."

SuAnn smiled sadly. "It's no big deal. There were just some anomalies on my blood work. They're going to retest it around Thanksgiving."

"What kind of anomalies?" Janine asked.

"I don't really understand all of that. But it could point to something concerning. We just are going to watch it for a while."

"Why are you being so evasive about this? Do you want us to just worry for the next few months? Why aren't we doing something sooner? I have a great doctor that I know in Atlanta…"

"Julie, I love Dr. Archer. He knows what he's doing. And I don't want to talk about this anymore. I just want you girls to do me this one favor. Spend some time together. Let Janine help you work on this house. She's got great design skills."

Julie struggled not to laugh. The last time she had seen Janine's design skills, it looked like a flower child had landed right in the middle of her bedroom. She definitely wasn't interested in that look for her cottage.

"What are you asking us to do?" Julie finally asked, worried about the answer.

"Let Janine stay here. Spend a few weeks together. Get past all of these issues that have kept you apart. Do you know what I would give to have my sister back? She died so young, and we were best friends . It breaks my heart that my own two daughters can't get along. When I'm gone, you are all you're going to have left."

"Mom, there's a lot of water under the bridge."

"I agree. I don't think our relationship is salvageable," Janine said, a hint of irritation in her voice.

"Julie, how would you feel if Meg and Colleen stopped speaking? What would it feel like at the holidays for you, as their mother?"

Julie stopped for a moment and thought about it. It would be heartbreaking. She loved her daughters so much, and they were so close. It would destroy the holidays if they weren't speaking or only one of them came to family functions. She couldn't believe what she was about to say.

"Fine. This is about new beginnings and taking chances, so I'm willing to take a chance on letting Janine stay here temporarily. Of course, she has to be willing."

Janine looked up at the ceiling and sighed. "I guess

anything is possible. So, yes, I'll stay here for a little while and we can see how it goes."

Neither woman looked particularly happy about their decision, but SuAnn was over the moon excited. She jumped up and down until she realized that the floor beneath her might give way and stopped, looking around her feet like she was about to be sucked up by a sinkhole.

"Oh, thank you, girls! You don't know how much this eases my mind. Now I can go home to my beloved Buddy and rest easy that both of you are taken care of."

Again, Julie got the feeling that something was going on with Janine she was unaware of.

"Janine, why don't you take your things and put them in the kitchen."

"The kitchen?"

"Well, as you can see I don't exactly have guest rooms set up. We'll figure it out after mom leaves. Let me just walk her out."

Janine nodded and walked toward the kitchen.

Julie pointed for her mother to join her on the front porch and closed the door behind them. When she was sure that Janine couldn't hear their conversation, she turned back to her mother.

"Okay, what's really going on?"

SuAnn cocked her head to the side like a dog who had heard a loud noise. "What do you mean?"

"You know what I mean. Something is obviously going on with Janine. You didn't just bring her here to help me. You're dumping her here, and I want to know why."

"I'm not dumping her. I just can't handle her anymore. She's been staying with me for six months now."

"And you're just now telling me this? What's going on with her?"

SuAnn took in a deep breath and sighed. "I can't say

anything. I don't want to betray her confidence. But your sister needs you right now, and if you were honest with yourself you would admit that you need her too. So I am giving you this time with her."

"Again, you're dumping her here. I didn't need another project, Mom."

"I can't believe you would say that about your own sister. What is wrong with you? You barely come around your family anymore. Buddy and I were talking about it just the other day."

"I barely know the man."

"That's because you don't come around. I'm trying to pull our family back together, Julie. I'm not getting any younger."

"Mom, please don't pull the age card on me. You've been doing that my whole life."

"Well, I am getting older and I don't know how long I'll be here. I'd like to see my daughters get along, even if it's just for my benefit."

Julie took a deep breath and blew it out slowly, trying everything she could to calm down. Her life had been such a whirlwind lately that she didn't even know which end was up. And her fight was getting weaker. She just didn't feel like arguing with her mother anymore.

"Fine. I will make my best effort, but I can't make any guarantees. There's a lot of history between me and Janine, and I honestly don't know how that can be fixed. But I will try if she will."

A smile spread across SuAnn's face. "That's my girl. I knew I could count on you. I'm going to head back up to see my beloved Buddy and rest easy knowing that both of my daughters are in good hands with each other."

She quickly hugged Julie, not something she did lightly, and trotted off to her car. As she pulled out of the driveway and down the long dirt road, Julie wondered what in the world she had gotten herself into.

When she walked back into the house, Janine was nowhere to be found. Had she already run away? Had she found a cute guy down by the marsh that Julie hadn't seen previously?

She walked toward the back deck and found her sister standing there, staring out into the murky abyss, her eyes closed. She was taking in a slow deep breath.

"Are you okay?"

Janine laughed softly. "I just had a very long drive with our mother. What do you think?"

"I can see your point. So, I guess I should give you an update on what's going on around here."

Janine turned around, and again Julie was taken with how she looked so different. Gone was the perfectly coiffed hair and the funky fashion choices. Instead, she looked very plain, with little make up. She was wearing a basic pair of blue jeans, a simple white T-shirt and sneakers. This wasn't the Janine she remembered.

"I bought this place sight unseen, obviously. I almost turned around and left when I got here but I ended up staying at what I thought was a little inn on the other end of the island for a night."

"You thought it was an inn? You mean, it wasn't?"

"Long story, but the man who owns the inn has offered to help me renovate this place for a really good deal."

"You mean he's interested in you."

"No, Janine, contrary to what you may think, not everything is about relationships with men."

"If there's one thing I know, it's that men don't do anything without a reason. He's interested in you. Or at least there's some ulterior motive."

"My, Janine, are you a bit jaded these days?"

"No. I just know how men are. You were married for too long. I just know that men don't do anything without a reason."

"Well, you can think what you want, but he's a nice guy and my only friend on the island, so I took him up on the offer. Absolutely nothing is going to happen. I'm done with men for a while, maybe forever."

Janine turned back around and looked at the marsh. "I see you're still a little overly dramatic."

"Look, I didn't invite you here, Janine. You were thrust upon me, so I'd really appreciate it if you could try to be nice."

"Me? Try to be nice? Are you serious right now?"

"What?"

"Julie, everybody knows I'm the nice one." Janine turned and walked back inside the house. Dawson was standing in the kitchen, sanding the baseboards on his hands and knees. He didn't look up.

"You're the nice one? Maybe flighty. Maybe strange. Perhaps loud and obnoxious. But nice? I don't think so."

Now, they were getting louder. These were the kinds of arguments that had gotten worse in their adult years. Yelling, screaming, name calling. It was embarrassing, but seemed necessary at the time.

"Obnoxious? I'm not the one who married the idiot who cheated on me with another woman and had a baby. Great picking skills you have there, sis."

"At least I was able to find a husband! You're an old maid!"

"Free. What I am is free. No strings. Happy."

"Yeah, you sure look happy," Julie retorted, rolling her eyes. Dawson rose to his feet slowly and slipped out the back door, obviously uncomfortable. She wouldn't be surprised if he walked back to his house and never showed up for work again.

Julie looked back at her sister. Janine was staring at her, tears rolling down her face, mouth clamped shut. Never, in all of their crazy arguments, had Janine shed a tear. Neither of them had, really. There was too much anger.

"Janine? What's wrong?" Her sisterly instinct told her to reach out and touch Janine, but she didn't.

"You're right. I'm not happy."

"I can see that."

"I've been living with Mom for six months, sleeping in the guest room amongst her craft supplies."

"What has happened to you, Janine?"

"Like you care." Janine walked over to the wall and slid down to the floor, her knees pulled to her chest. She stared straight ahead.

Julie didn't know what to say or do. She just froze in place for a moment, fully aware that her only sister was in a lump on the floor. She slowly walked over and sat down a few feet away, pulling her knees up too.

"I do care."

"Yeah, right. I bet you fought Mom tooth and nail to keep her from leaving me here."

Julie paused. "It still doesn't mean that I don't care."

"Trust me, I didn't want to come here in the first place."

"Then why did you? Did she guilt trip you too?"

"No. She kicked me out."

Julie looked at her. "What? Kicked you out? For what reason?"

Janine sighed. "For having problems. You know how our mother likes to keep up appearances. I was apparently embarrassing her."

"How were you embarrassing her?"

"I wasn't you."

"What?"

"You've always been her favorite, Julie. You know that."

"Actually, I've always thought the opposite."

Janine looked over, her head tilted. "Seriously? Mom always bragged on you, even posted on social media a few times about your perfect little family."

"That was just to impress her friends at the country club."

"Right. And nothing I've ever done has impressed her."

"So, you're telling me she kicked you out because you weren't up to her standards? Come on, Janine, she's not that bad. There has to be more to this story."

Janine turned her head and stared off into space, something that seemed to be typical for her now. The bubbly, vivacious, take no prisoners personality that she'd had her entire life seemed to be gone, gobbled up by what appeared to be depression or something similar.

"The last couple of years have been difficult. I've had some real struggles, and when I couldn't make it on my own anymore, I turned to my mother. She tried to help, in her own 'SuAnn way', but I think she just couldn't take seeing me like this anymore. So, she told me we were coming to see you. I didn't want to come, but she packed my bag and told me that I could no longer stay with her. I didn't have anywhere else to go."

"So you don't have a job or anything?"

"I haven't had a job in a couple of years. Like I said, I've had some difficulties."

Julie stood up and put her hands on her hips. "Janine, you're too old for this. Why don't you have a job? You need to be able to support yourself. I'm sorry, but you can't just live here without working or contributing ."

Janine put her face in her hands. "This isn't about being lazy, Julie. I can't function very well right now."

"I don't understand. It seems like both you and Mom aren't telling me something, and I deserve to know, especially if you want to stay at my house for free. I mean I'm right in the middle of a remodel. I can't take on another mouth to feed when I can barely afford myself."

"If I had anywhere else to go, trust me, I would!" Janine stood up, and it was the first bit of energy Julie had seen out of her since she arrived.

"You know, you've been like this your whole life. You expect to just be able to galavant all over the world and do whatever you want to do and everybody else has to pick up the pieces. Well you know what? Life isn't like that! Life is hard! You have to work and be an adult!"

Tears streamed down Janine's face again. "You're right. This is all my fault. It's totally my fault that I was attacked."

"Attacked?"

"Two years ago. I was in the Caribbean, teaching yoga at this little place near a resort. One night, after a class, I was walking to my bungalow that I rented. I didn't make it there."

Julie felt like her insides were caving in. She couldn't take a breath. The image of her sister being attacked in a foreign country with no one to help her made her feel like her guts were being ripped out.

"I had no idea."

"Nobody else knows."

"Wait. Mom doesn't know?"

"No. That's not exactly the kind of thing I want to talk to her about. Plus, she would find a way to blame it on me. And, honestly, I blame it on me."

"Janine, it's not your fault. No person deserves to be attacked."

"Maybe I did. I wasn't paying attention. I trusted my surroundings. I had been there for over six months, and I just wasn't careful. I left my mace at home..."

Julie walked over to her sister and put her hands on her upper arms. "Janine, this is not your fault. And I think you should tell Mom. I'm sure she would let you stay there if she knew."

"Julie, I don't want to tell her. There's nothing she can do about it. And it wouldn't make her understand what I'm going through any more than she does right now. I think she kind of knows something happened, but I don't really think she wants to know the details."

Julie stepped back. "You're probably right. Have you had any counseling?"

"Unemployed people don't really have access to health insurance or money for counselors. Mom kept pushing me to get a real job, told me to stop teaching yoga to hippies."

Julie chuckled. "That sounds like Mom."

"Over time, I started to treat the trauma my own way."

Julie looked at her sister, and it dawned on her. "Do you have an eating disorder, Janine?"

"Is it that obvious?"

"To me it is. You have to get some help. This could be life-threatening."

"Look, I know you don't want me to stay here any more than I want to be here. But, maybe this could be a fresh start for me. At least I can be here to help you get this place in order. Maybe that will help get me out of my funk."

"You can stay here. But, this is more than just a funk. You have to get help. We will find you a counselor on the mainland."

"I can't afford that, Julie. And I don't think you can either."

"We will figure it out. I know we haven't been close since we were kids, but you're still my sister, and I'm going to help you."

Janine smiled sadly. "I hope I'm not beyond help."

"Nobody is beyond help. Well, except for maybe my ex-husband."

And that was the first time she saw Janine truly smile.

CHAPTER 7

*J*ulie walked outside and sat down on a wrought iron bench near the marsh's edge. It was the only place she'd found where she could truly be alone with her thoughts. Janine had helped her clean more of the house, and they'd set up a makeshift bedroom they could share until Dawson had gotten more of the work done. Sharing a room with her sister again when they were both in their 40's wasn't something she'd exactly had on her bucket list.

She'd also had a long talk with her daughter, Colleen, about her actions. Telling her mother where she was and what was really going on wasn't her place, but Julie could hardly be mad at her. She missed her too much.

"You okay?" she heard Dawson say from behind her.

"Oh, hey. I thought you'd already left for the day. It's almost supper time, isn't it?"

He walked closer and stood at the end of the bench. "I ate a sandwich from my cooler an hour or so ago."

"Go home, Dawson. Enjoy your evening."

"Mind if I sit for a minute before I go?"

She smiled and patted the seat next to her. "Sorry you had to hear all that craziness earlier."

"That's why I wanted to check and see if you were good."

She chuckled. "No, I'm not good yet. Maybe one day I will be. But, I'm okay, and that's enough for right now."

"So, that's your sister?"

"Yes. That's my sister. As you can tell, we've had a tumultuous history with each other."

"Seems that way," he said, a quirk of a smile on his face. He kicked a mound of stray moss with his boot, sending it closer to the water's edge.

"We were close as kids, but we're just so different."

"Different how?"

"How long do you have?" she asked with a laugh.

"As long as you need," he said, sending chills up her back that she hadn't expected. There was no doubt this guy was handsome, like some kind of Southern god that had risen up from the marshy waters beyond. But, she was nowhere close to falling in love again. Michael's so-called love had wrecked her heart.

"Janine is what you'd probably call a 'free spirit'. As long as I can remember, she did what she wanted without a care in the world. She believed in magic and fairies and unicorns, hung out with the strangest people and just wouldn't settle down. She traveled the world, teaching yoga, burning incense and trying to save the planet. Meanwhile, I had the typical little white picket fence life in suburbia with my husband and two kids."

"Yeah, but people are different all the time. Why don't you two get along?"

"When we were kids, it was fun having a quirky sister. But as we got older, she just wasn't there for me. She was always traveling, and I was lucky to get a postcard. I guess I just got used to my soccer mom lifestyle. I got used to not having her around."

"I had a brother like that. He worked on Wall Street, of all things. Stock trader."

"Past tense?"

"He died a few years ago. Heart attack from all the stress. That's when I decided I wasn't leaving this island. There's no stress on Seagrove."

"My sister may have brought it," Julie said with a tired laugh.

"So did you have a falling out?"

"Somewhat. Janine came back around more when my girls were young. She started visiting, but when I learned that she was giving life advice to my teenagers, I had to put my foot down. She'd almost convinced my oldest to join the Peace Corps."

"And that was bad?"

Julie shrugged her shoulders. "I guess I had this vision in my mind of my daughters going to college, getting married, raising families of their own. Janine giving them life advice wasn't what I wanted."

"Because you wanted them to be like you and not like her," he said, matter-of-factly.

Julie was offended. "No, that wasn't it at all. I just didn't like the advice she was giving them."

"Sorry. I didn't mean to upset you."

"It's fine. I'm just a little raw lately. I didn't mean to snap at you."

Dawson stood and smoothed out his jeans. "Look, I don't want to step on any toes, but can I give you a little piece of advice?"

"Of course."

"Life is very short, and it sounds like you're getting a

second chance with your only sister. Don't waste it. I wish I had a second chance with my brother."

Julie nodded. "I get what you mean."

"Goodnight, Julie," he said, before walking toward the front of the house.

She stared back over the marsh, and watched the sun rapidly descend below the horizon, leaving trails of orange and pink in the sky. As she walked back toward the house, she thought about how her life was now a series of new beginnings. Divorced. New house. New male friend who she was determined would remain only a friend. And now her sister.

How in the world would she handle this new life of hers?

~

IT WAS pitch black dark when Julie walked back into the house. Her sister was sitting in their makeshift bedroom, a candle lit and her eyes closed as she sat on the floor in a cross legged position.

This was more like the Janine she knew. She was probably meditating to some higher power. As long as she didn't start chanting or summoning spirits, Julie decided to leave her alone. She walked back to the kitchen in search of something to eat for dinner, grabbing a battery powered lantern on her way.

"I wasn't meditating, by the way," Janine suddenly said from behind her.

"I didn't ask," Julie said as she continued to rummage around in her cooler and bags. With two of them to feed, she would have to go back for more supplies in a couple days.

"I was just doing some breathing. Lots of stress today. I don't think it really helps me anymore like it used to."

"Sorry to hear that."

"Is this how it's going to be? Me talking and you giving me short answers?"

"Janine, I don't know what you want me to say. I'm not exactly an expert in meditation or deep breathing."

Julie pulled frozen beans and a box of macaroni and cheese out of her supplies. She had purchased a small charcoal grill and a couple of pots. She dragged it all out onto the deck and started assembling what she needed to cook the beans and the macaroni and cheese. She had to get electricity in this house and pronto.

"Look, I know you don't know a whole lot about my life and what I've been doing all these years. I know you never really got into the whole yoga and meditation thing either. But I haven't done that in a couple of years because it just doesn't seem to fit me anymore."

Julie looked up at her as she worked on lighting the grill. "I'm surprised to hear that. You always loved stretching your body into those crazy positions.

"Yes, I did. But after I was attacked, it just seemed so trivial. The one thing that was a constant in my life for all those years just didn't seem to help me. The grief and the pain of that just overwhelmed me to the point that I couldn't even do yoga anymore. I lost the last job I had because I would burst into tears during class. Of course, nobody knew what had happened to me, so I can't really blame them for sending me on my way."

"Tomorrow I have to go into town to get more supplies. While I'm there, I'll do some asking around and see what resources they have for someone going through trauma."

"It's already enough that you're letting me stay here. I can't ask you to pay for counseling for me."

Julie stood and looked at her sister. "You didn't ask me. I'm offering. As much as you're weird and quirky personality has irritated me in the past, I want you to feel better. Nobody should feel stuck like this."

"Thank you. You'll never know how much I appreciate everything."

"If you want to show me your appreciation, help me figure out what the heck I'm doing wrong with this grill!"

Janine laughed as she bent down and began working on lighting the grill.

~

THE NEXT MORNING, Julie woke up later than usual. It had been a long night with her sister in the room. She had repeated nightmares that caused her to wake up screaming multiple times. Julie felt like she had a toddler again as she soothed her sister back to sleep over and over. One thing was for sure, she needed help. And Julie was pretty angry with her own mother for not doing something sooner. It was obvious that Janine needed professional assistance, and she couldn't understand why their mother hadn't gotten her some help.

She walked down the hall, the smell of coffee wafting into her nose. Dawson was standing in the kitchen, a full pot of coffee sitting on the counter behind him.

"Is this a mirage? Is that actual, real life coffee sitting there?"

He laughed. "You don't think that a contractor can work without coffee, do you?"

"But we don't have any electricity here. How did you manage this miraculous feat?"

"Well, that's the beauty of a generator. I've got one plugged in on the other side of this window. And don't worry, I have set you up to get electricity run sometime this week."

"Thank God. I never liked camping, And I think this might be worse."

"Cream and sugar?"

"Yes, please."

He made her cup of coffee and handed it to her. She had never been so happy to receive a drink in all her life. "Have you seen my sister this morning?"

"She was walking down the street when I pulled in."

Julie's eyes widened. "Walking down the street? And you didn't stop her?"

"Why would I stop her? The island is the safest place on earth."

"Not for my sister. She's going through a really difficult time right now. Plus there's alligators and I don't know what else lurks out in those swamp waters."

"First of all, it's a marsh, not a swamp. Big difference. Secondly, your sister is a grown woman. I'm sure she's just getting the lay of the land and maybe clearing her mind."

"Still, I better get out there and look for her," Julie said, setting her cup on the counter and heading for the front door.

"Wait, I'll come with you," he said, following behind her.

They walked out onto the front porch and Julie looked up and down the road. The island wasn't that big, so she was sure they'd be able to find her quickly.

"Janine! Janine!" she called. They walked around the house and then back to the front again. She was nowhere to be found.

"Now I'm getting worried. I can't believe she just walked off like this."

"I'm sure she'll be back. Why don't we give her a little time to herself. If she's not back in an hour, then we'll hop in my truck and go looking for her."

"Okay. One hour. But if she's not back by then, we go searching."

"I promise," Dawson said.

They went back into the house, but Julie only made it about thirty minutes before she found herself looking out all of the windows again. Dawson continued working on whatever it was he was doing, but all she could think about was her sister. Hurt, lost, traumatized.

"I've got to go looking for her," Julie said.

"We've got thirty more minutes…"

"Look, my sister is going through some things. I'm not going to talk about it, but I'm worried about her mental health right now. I need to find her."

"Okay, I understand. Let me take you," Dawson said.

They jumped into his truck and started driving down the road. Julie was looking side to side, trying desperately to see if her sister was lost or hurt in some way. Visions of her being eaten by an alligator or pecked to death by one of those large birds she'd seen popped into her mind. She had always been a worry wart at heart.

"Why don't we drive over to the beach side. I have a feeling she might have gone that way," Dawson said.

Julie didn't answer and just kept looking out the window hoping that she would see her picking flowers or petting a dog or something simple like that.

They pulled up to the beach, an area that she hadn't been since moving there, and Dawson told her to follow him down a pathway. It was all white sand and flanked by large beach grass. When they stepped onto the actual beach, Julie stopped for a moment and stared. The beauty of the place was undeniable. Although she wished her house was on the beach side, she was excited to know it was so close. It hadn't crossed her mind that she had fulfilled her own dream of living at the beach by moving there. Everything had been so stressful so far, she hadn't taken a moment to be grateful for the fact that she was living at the beach. It was just a short drive down the road.

But right now all she could think about was her sister. What if she had come to the beach and somehow got sucked out by riptide and...

"Isn't that her over there?" Dawson said, pointing off in the distance. Sure enough, Janine was sitting atop a large rock outcropping that was partially submerged in water.

"Yes. What in the world is she doing?" Julie ranted as she walked quickly towards her sister. Dawson stayed back, obviously not wanting to get into the fray.

"Janine!" Julie called as she got closer. Janine was sitting there, her knees pulled to her chest, staring off into the water, her curly locks blowing in the breeze. She was wearing a long white skirt and a white tank top and looked angelic, but right now Julie wanted to wring her neck.

"What are you doing here?" Janine asked, like it was the most natural thing in the world that she had left home without telling Julie and had gone to sit on a rock in the ocean.

"What am I doing here? What are *you* doing here? You didn't even tell me you were leaving."

Janine cocked her head to the side. "I didn't know I needed permission, *Mom*."

"See? This is exactly what I'm talking about. You do things without any thought for how they affect other people!"

"Me walking to the beach on a tiny island affected you? You were asleep. I didn't want to wake you up. I kept you up all night with my nightmares, and I was trying to let you get some rest. So, I got up this morning and decided to come out here and just enjoy the ocean breeze."

"You could've at least left a note."

"Oh yes, with all the stationary and pens you have in the house? Come on, Julie, this isn't a big deal."

Julie shook her head. "Nothing is ever a big deal to you, Janine. Unless it involves you. But no, if it involves other people, you have no cares in the world."

Janine climbed down from the rock and stood in front of her sister. "You're not being fair. I took a walk. You live at the beach. I figured you could connect those dots without a problem."

"Don't be sarcastic."

"Look, Julie, I appreciate what you're doing for me. I truly do. But, I don't need you to be my mother hen.

"I'm worried about you. There, I said it. I'm worried."

"I'm not going to harm myself. And believe it or not, after traveling all over the world *alone*, I know how to take care of myself too. I can walk a quarter of a mile to the beach and sit on a rock without being murdered or eaten by a pack of wolves."

Julie chuckled. "Alligators. I wasn't worried about wolves."

Janine smiled. "I know we have a checkered past, but this feels like a new beginning for both of us, in more ways than one. Can we just agree to let some of that stuff go? Maybe try to give each other a break?"

"I am trying. I know you may not believe that, but I really am."

CHAPTER 8

*D*riving onto the mainland was like going to another country, even after just a couple of days on the island. Still, Julie much preferred the slower pace of island life as she watched the cars whizzing by on the street in front of her.

She was lost. Majorly lost. She had only gone to the store once before, to get her supplies. But that was an accidental finding, and now she had to get her bearings to figure out where she was all over again.

She pulled down a one way street and into a parking space so she could get out and look around. Surely, there was a big box store somewhere.

"You lost, hon?" She heard a woman say behind her. She turned to see a most unusual lady, Southern to her core, for sure.

She was wearing red pants with what appeared to be parrots all over them, a white tank top with a ruffled neckline and the biggest sun hat Julie had ever seen, complete with a large flower on the side of it. And her accent was right out of Gone With The Wind, thick with Southern gentility and a little rough around the edges at the same time.

"Actually, yes. I'm looking for a grocery store."

"Oh, sugar, you're about two miles in the wrong direction. You aren't from around here, are ya?" Her voice was like a warm blanket from the past.

"No, ma'am, I'm not. Just moved over to Seagrove Island this week."

"I see. Beautiful, little island, but a bit wild."

"I agree with that characterization," Julie said, smiling.

"Pardon me for saying so, sweetie, but you look rode hard and put away wet."

Julie stared at her. "I'm sorry, but I don't really know what that means."

"Are you from up north?"

"No. Atlanta."

"Goodness, what has happened to Atlantans? Ya'll don't know all the good Southern sayings? We'll have to remedy that," she said with a chuckle. "Follow me."

"I... uh..." Julie stammered as she looked between the woman and her car.

"Don't worry. I own these parking spaces, so you won't get towed. Plus, Billy at the towing company would come ask me first anyhow."

She started walking away, and for some reason Julie felt obligated to follow her. She was still lost, and this woman seemed to be her only connection to this place at the moment.

"I'm Dixie, by the way," she said as they walked, reaching her perfectly manicured hand over to Julie. She had big gaudy rings on just about every finger, and the veins in her hands were thick and ropy, much like she remembered of her own grandmother.

"Julie," she said as they stopped in front of a small shop.

"This here is my bookstore. Come on inside and sit a spell," she said, like she was right out of some Southern movie.

Julie followed her inside and her mouth dropped open. Never had she been inside of a more authentic bookstore than this one. Back in Atlanta, she'd only gone into chain bookstores, each one looking the same with high ceilings, bright fluorescent lights and the same books and displays.

But this place looked like one of a kind with walls of books, little space to walk and even a scruffy little dog laying in the front entrance, taking in the bits of sunlight gleaming through the plate glass window.

"Wow, this place is amazing. How long have you owned it?"

"I opened when my boys were knee high to a grasshopper, and that was a long time ago."

Julie smiled. "I might need a Southern dictionary to talk to you, Miss Dixie."

"Please just call me Dixie. I'm already older than dirt, no need to make me feel worse about it," she said with a loud laugh. "And to answer your question, I opened this place over twenty years ago. My sons were in high school at the time, so maybe I fibbed a little about the grasshopper part."

"Dixie!" A woman called out as she came into the store.

"Excuse me a second, hon. Feel free to browse around if ya like."

Dixie got up and ran to hug the woman. They chatted for a while as Julie walked around the small store. The dog, whose tag said Rhett, followed her around, occasionally licking her ankles.

She could smell the books. You couldn't really smell books in chain bookstores. They smelled more like coffee and high prices.

But this place was like something out of another time.

Sitting between a barber shop and an antique store, it was nestled in safety from being gobbled up by big business.

There was a whole section of Gone With The Wind books and memorabilia, much like a shrine. She took it that Dixie was a fan, especially given that the resident dog was named Rhett.

"Sorry about that, darlin'. That was one of my regular customers."

"No problem. I see you're a fan of Gone With The Wind?"

Dixie laughed. "My late husband was, actually. This is kind of my shrine for him. But I have to admit, I do love me some Rhett Butler."

"What is the name of this place?"

"Down Yonder Books," she said, opening her arms like she was on stage.

"Of course it is," Julie said with a giggle.

"Care for some sweet tea?"

"I don't really drink sweet tea. Do you have unsweetened?"

"Sacrilege! Honey, we don't serve anything here without sugar. That's what sweetens up your life!"

Dixie walked toward the front and poured two large glasses of sweet tea, totally ignoring Julie's comments. She sat down at one of the three bistro tables and pointed to the chair across from her.

"Come sit. Tell me all the good stuff about your life, Julie."

"Okay, but then I really have to get going to the grocery store."

Julie sat down. "Life is slower down in these parts, my dear. The grocery store can wait a bit, can't it? Help an old lady not feel so lonely and tell me something about yourself."

"I have a feeling you're the least lonely person in this town," Julie said with a chuckle.

"Just 'cause people come around doesn't mean I'm not lonely."

"Sorry for the wrong assumption then. Let's see, what can I tell you about myself?" Julie said before taking a sip of tea without thinking. She almost spit it right back out, the ropiness causing her tastebuds to rebel. Not wanting to offend, she swallowed it down anyway, feeling sure she could feel the grittiness of the sugar sliding down her throat. "I'm newly divorced."

"Scoundrel of a husband?"

Julie laughed. "How'd you know?"

"There's three kinds of husbands, in my unbiased opinion. Good ones, scoundrels and dead ones." She broke out in hysterical laughter and slapped Julie's hand across the table.

"I think I agree with you on that one," Julie said, taking another sip. Maybe she was becoming more Southern by the minute because this time it didn't seem so bad.

"So what did this scoundrel do?"

"He cheated on me after over twenty years of marriage. And got her pregnant. And now they're getting married."

"Good Lord, he is a scoundrel! Well, she better remember that what they'll do with you, they'll do to you. Her time is coming." Julie found it funny that Dixie said the same thing she'd said to Victoria's face in the parking lot.

"Maybe so. We were supposed to buy a beach house now that our kids are grown and gone. Instead, I ended up on the island with a cottage on the marsh that is in complete shambles."

"Oh, I bet I know the one. Has blue shutters?"

"Yes! How did you know?"

"My old friends lived there for a long time. You've met Dawson then?"

"This is spooky. How do you know Dawson?"

"Sugar, we all know each other around here! Dawson

grew up with my sons. They all went to school together, and they sure got in trouble a few times too."

"Oh yeah? Dawson seems so put together now."

"Age does that to a person, I 'spose. But I remember the time he snuck out in the middle of the night and got caught skinny dipping in the ocean with a Trina Cox. Man, she was something else. I think she dances on one of those poles somewhere in Alabama now."

"In her forties?"

"I didn't say she had a lot of business," Dixie said, a deadpan look on her face. Julie laughed.

"You're quite a character, Dixie. I'm glad you found me wandering around out there. I've felt a bit lost since moving here last week. Dawson is my one friend."

"Well, he's a good one."

"Yes, he is. And he's also my contractor."

"Good choice. He'll get you fixed up, for sure."

"Well, I really should get to the store. My sister is staying with me, and we're going to be awfully hungry."

"You're mighty lucky to have a sister. I'm an only child, and it sure makes for a lonely life sometimes."

"No grandkids?"

"No. My youngest son died when he was twenty-three."

"Oh my goodness! I'm so sorry."

"I'd like to say it gets easier as the years pass, but I'd be lyin'. I miss him every single day, and I still cry from time to time."

"Can I ask what happened?"

"Hunting accident with his Daddy. Poor Johnny, he was never the same again."

"And your older son?"

"Haven't heard from him in over ten years. I've tried, but he won't respond. I think he lives in Tennessee. He just wasn't the same after losing his brother and Dad. Blamed me for his Daddy dying."

"Oh wow. I am so sorry, Dixie."

"Johnny had cancer. My son, William, well, he just thought I should have made him get treatment. Johnny didn't want treatment. He didn't want to be sick for the time he had left. William thought I should force the issue, and I wouldn't. A person should have a right to make their own choice, ya know?"

"I agree. So he just stopped speaking?"

"Yep. He told me off after the funeral and took off. No cards or letters or anything."

"That must be hard. I can't imagine never speaking to my daughters again."

"So you can see why the loneliness is always there, even when people are around."

Suddenly, Julie felt so bad for Dixie. Here was this amazing, flamboyant, outgoing woman, running an adorable book store and she was lonely, even though everyone probably loved her to pieces.

Life was cruel sometimes.

Dixie stood up, brushed off her pants - even though nothing was on them - and walked to the counter. She pulled a map from a plastic box and grabbed a pen.

"We get lots of tourists in these parts, so I keep maps on hand." She opened the map on the table and drew a series of lines and then circled the nearest grocery store. "You're not too far off. Just take this road here, and when you see the gas station, take a right…"

"Thank you so much, Dixie. For the map and for the company. And if you're ever on the island, you know where I am. Please come by. I'd love to return the favor."

"I'll keep that in mind. I do like to sit by the marsh from time to time. It soothes my old, weary soul."

"Well, you're always welcome," Julie said as she grasped both of Dixie's hands and smiled.

"Thanks for sitting with me."

Julie walked toward the door. "Oh, can I ask you one more thing?"

"Of course."

"Do you know of any counseling services around town? For someone who went through trauma?"

"You okay, hon? What else did that scoundrel do?"

"No, it's not for me. My sister needs some... help."

Dixie nodded knowingly. "I see. There's a wonderful free counseling center down on Eller Street. Here's a card," she said, pulling a card off of a huge bulletin board behind her cash register.

"Thank you so much."

"No problem. And welcome to town."

"I think I'm going to love it here," Julie said. And she really believed it.

CHAPTER 9

"*E*lectricity? Is this real? Am I dead? Should I go toward the light?" Julie said, spinning around in the living room as she looked at the light shining above her.

"Real as it gets," Dawson said, a lazy smile on his face.

"You're a miracle worker."

"Actually, the power company guy was the miracle worker. I just let him in."

"It's really starting to come together, isn't it? I mean, this might actually turn into a real house?" She could hardly believe she finally felt hopeful again. She had a great contractor who was also a friend, she had groceries, the beach was close, she was working on getting along with her sister and now she had lights. And air conditioning!

She'd never been so happy to have the basics in life. Before, it was all about the high end oven she'd bought for her gourmet kitchen. Now, it was about the wind up lantern she'd found half off at the hardware store. Sometimes, life sure could take a crazy turn.

Still, there were moments she found herself overwhelmed. Sometimes, she shed a few tears thinking about her marriage falling apart, wishing against reality that Michael was there to hold her close and make her feel safe. More than anything, she missed that feeling, the one where she knew someone had her back.

"If you don't mind, I'm going to leave a little early today. I have a couple of projects around the inn that require a bit of daylight. Do you mind?"

"Are you kidding me? Dawson, you've been here morning until night since you began. Take whatever time you need."

"Thanks. I'm going to get started on painting the living room first thing tomorrow."

"Great. I can't wait to start decorating at least one room in this place."

"Enjoy your electricity tonight," he said, smiling as he picked up his well worn toolbox and headed to the door.

"Oh, trust me, I will. As soon as Janine gets back from her counseling group, we're going to have a 'thank God for Ben Franklin' party!"

Dawson chuckled as he shut the door behind him.

Julie walked out onto the deck. She stood there, staring into the marsh, the large blades of grass blowing in the breeze. It was still light for another couple of hours, so she took a moment to take in the sights and smells of her new home.

Michael would've hated this. He wasn't a huge fan of the beach, but the marsh may have done him in. The thought of it made her smile.

He hated dirt. He was never one of those guys who liked to get in the mud or have dirt under his nails. Basically, he was totally the opposite of Dawson.

Sometimes, she marveled as she watched Dawson work. He was a man, through and through, but there was a sensitivity about him that one wouldn't expect when they met him. He was deep, but in a way that wasn't weird or woo-woo. It was just who he was.

He could hold a conversation and a hammer, something she might not have thought was all that special a few weeks ago.

Michael had hired people to hang the pictures in their home. He'd paid a lawn maintenance company, a pool company and even had a special company that came out once a year to clean all of the vents in their home. In fact, she couldn't remember one thing he'd ever done that would be classified as work around their house. The most he'd done was break down Amazon boxes and put them by the road for the garbage man.

How hadn't she noticed that about him for all those years? She'd changed all the diapers, helped with the girls' school projects, run them to and from almost every event. Michael had been like a fixture that was there, but maybe he never was. Perhaps she'd been more invested in their marriage than he had all those years.

Something about this island was pulling memories out of her brain that she'd long since forgotten, like the time he'd come home from a business trip smelling like perfume. When she'd questioned him, he'd brushed it off by saying the woman in one of his meetings had doused herself and almost choked everyone else in the conference room. Now she wondered if that was even true. Did Victoria smell like perfume when she met her? She searched her mind, but couldn't remember.

"The lights are on?" she heard Janine say from behind her, a giddy sound in her voice.

"Yep!" Julie said, slightly jumping up and down as she clapped her hands. "Can you believe it?"

Janine laughed. "I don't think you'd make a very good camper."

Julie leaned against the railing. "Oh, and you would?"

"Um, yeah. Remember, I've traveled all over the world, and to some very remote places. I've stayed in tents and teepees and a few times just right out under the moon, lying on the grass."

Julie rolled her eyes. "Of course you have."

"Why did you say it like that?"

"Because you've had the most adventurous life. I'm sure mine pales by comparison."

"I've never said that, Julie. The only person saying that is you."

"Fine. Let's not do this right now. I don't want to ruin my good mood. The lights are on, the air is blowing, and I just want to bask in the miracle that it is. So, how did your group counseling go?"

Janine's face fell a bit. "Okay, I guess. I'm still not sure it's for me."

"You're not quitting are you?" Julie asked, a little more accusatory than she meant to sound.

Janine paused. "No. Not yet, anyway. I'll give it more time."

"Good." Julie looked around her sister into the open sliding glass door. "I think I want Dawson to replace this with French doors. What do you think?"

Janine turned to look. "Is that in the budget?"

The two women walked back into the house. Julie looked around and took in all that still needed to be done.

"Nothing else is really in the budget. I've been thinking about getting a job."

"A job? You?"

"Really? You're going to question me about jobs? You, who has been flitting all around the world for years?"

"Um, I was working most of the time, Julie."

"Teaching yoga." Julie didn't know why she was so insistent on poking at her sister about being a yoga teacher. It wasn't like there was anything wrong with that in general. It was just the idea of Janine wearing her tie dye yoga pants, saying her mantra, rolling her eyes back in her head as if she was summoning spirits from the great beyond.

All Julie could see was her sister, the one who wouldn't stop picking her nose when they were kids. The one who kept her room like a pig sty and was terrified of grasshoppers, of all things.

It was hard to see her as some kind of professional, someone who actually knew things. Or maybe it was because she felt less than, like she hadn't really lived. How she'd played it safe, and now she was left alone because of it.

"Teaching yoga is a job, whether you want to believe it or not, Julie."

"Okay. You're right." She threw her hands up, and walked toward the kitchen for a bottle of water. Her refrigerator, newly delivered that morning, was nice and cold already. Seriously, electricity is amazing.

"I don't think you believe me."

"What does it matter, Janine?" she said, taking a long sip.

"It matters to me that my sister knows what I do for a living."

"Did." Julie knew she shouldn't have said it. Rubbing her sister's forced break from her career in her face wasn't nice. It was downright mean, actually.

"Thanks a lot," Janine said, turning to walk to the bedroom.

"Janine, wait," Julie called, chasing her through the living room. "I didn't mean that. I'm sorry."

Janine stopped in her tracks and then turned around. "I

can't help what happened to me. You said it wasn't my fault. Did you even mean that?"

Julie felt horrible. "Of course I meant it. Truly. I'm just stressed and tired right now. How can I make it right?"

Janine thought for a moment and then smiled mischievously, much like she had when they were kids. "You can do a yoga class with me."

"What?"

"A yoga class."

"Where?"

"Right here, right now." She immediately started moving things out of the way, pushing stray supplies and trash to the edges of the wall.

"No... I'm really tired..."

Janine squeezed her arm. "Then yoga is perfect for you right now. It will rejuvenate you and help you sleep later." She turned and ran down the hall, reappearing with a yoga mat and a towel. "I'll use the towel."

"Janine..."

"Stop overthinking. Let me show you what I can do, and what yoga can do."

Julie paused. "Fine. But just for a few minutes. It's dinner time."

Janine grinned bigger than she'd seen her during the whole visit. "Yay! Okay, we'll start with mountain pose. Basically, you want to feel your feet grounded into the floor as we reconnect with Mother Earth..."

Julie rolled her eyes. "Mother Earth?"

"Fine. I'll keep the woo woo out of it for your benefit."

"Thank you."

"Okay, so stand with your feet like this and press down through your toes..."

They went through pose after pose until Julie was almost

a puddle in the floor. She couldn't believe her sister moved so easily through them all, like a lithe cat-like creature. Her bones and muscles bent and twisted in ways Julie couldn't have imagined before. When they were finished, Janine sat cross legged on the floor while Julie fell backward, her arms stretched to her sides and her chest heaving up and down.

"Good Lord, that is tougher than it looks! Was that intermediate or advanced stuff?"

Janine giggled. "That's what I teach in my beginner's class."

Julie cackled with laughter. "You're lying!"

"No, I'm not! I've had old ladies do that class in Bali!"

"Bali? What was that like?" Julie asked, sitting up and fanning her face.

"Heaven on Earth. Seriously, my favorite place I've lived."

"What about the summer you spent in Italy?"

"I've never eaten so much in my life. I taught yoga in this little village. It was so cute, and the people were so nice."

"I wish I had stories to tell," Julie said, sadly.

"You do have stories, Julie. About family. And that matters."

"I suppose so."

"I'm serious. I've enjoyed my life, most of the time. But I do regret not settling down and having a family. I guess time just got away from me."

"Really? You regret it? I always figured you just didn't want kids."

Janine stood up and walked to the kitchen. She opened the refrigerator and grabbed two pre-made salads Julie had bought at the store, bringing them back to her sister.

"I always wanted kids, but I never met the right guy."

Julie took one of the salads and popped open the plastic lid. She emptied the contents of the Italian dressing packet and removed the plastic fork from it's wrapper.

"You still have plenty of time to find the right man."

"Maybe, but my time to have a child is in the past."

Julie finished chewing. "You never know what life has in store. I mean, did you ever think we'd be living together in our forties, sitting on the floor of my money pit eating salad out of plastic boxes?"

Janine giggled. "We're truly living the dream, aren't we?"

"Yes, we are. No doubt about it. And if you really want to live the dream, then you can spend the rest of the evening helping me paint this room."

Janine stopped eating, her mouth dropping open. "You know how much I hate to paint."

"Well, it's not exactly the thing I love most in this world either. Dawson is supposed to do it tomorrow, but maybe I can save myself a little money if he doesn't have to do it."

Janine glared at her, squinting her eyes. "Fine. But only because you're letting me stay here rent free right now. Otherwise, I would pack my things and head off down the road at the mere mention of painting."

They finished up eating their salads and then started prepping the living room to be painted. Janine taped off the molding while Julie opened the paint can and stirred it. In reality, she hadn't done much painting in her life, but it seemed to be pretty cut and dry. Surely the two of them could figure it out.

They laid down drop cloths that Dawson had folded in the corner. Julie also found some contraption that Dawson must've left. It looked like a paint roller on a long stick but it had a tube inside. She figured that must've been where the paint needed to be poured in, so she decided to do it by herself.

"You better be careful with..." Janine started to say as Julie tried to pour paint from the big can into the tiny tube.

Within seconds, paint was running down the side of the stick onto the hardwood floors.

"Oh no!" she said, dropping everything onto a nearby drop cloth as she got on her hands and knees and tried to use the towel from their yoga practice to clean up the paint. All she was doing was smearing it everywhere.

"What are you doing? I think you're making it worse!" Janine said.

"No, really? Why don't you tell me something I didn't know?" Julie said, sarcastically.

Janine put her hands on her hips, something she had done since they were little kids. "Do you want my help or not?"

"No, I much prefer you stand there, staring at me with your hands on your hips. Can you at least give me some wet paper towels?"

This is how it always went. The two of them could never do any task without getting into an argument within a few moments. It was one of the reasons why Julie had never tried to mend the relationship until now. It was too much work, too many arguments about stupid little things. They never really argued about what was truly under the surface.

"Here." Janine said, handing her a couple of paper towels that were saturated with water.

"Do you think I'm going to be able to clean up all of this paint with this tiny wad of paper towels? Never mind, I'll get it myself."

Julie stood up and jogged to the kitchen, grabbing a large roll of paper towels and a cup of water.

"You could've told me exactly what you wanted. I would've brought it to you," Janine said, irritated.

"I thought you could figure it out. You're a grown woman."

"Well, you're a grown woman too, and I can see that

you're no better at communicating than you were when we were kids. Maybe that's what happened between you..." she stopped short, putting her hand over her mouth. It was obvious she knew she had gone too far.

Julie stood up to face her sister, her jaw twitching as her teeth ground together.

"Oh, I see. Do you think my marriage fell apart because I can't communicate? Not because my husband decided to snuggle up with a skank in Boston?"

"I didn't mean that. I was just mad."

"I think you did mean it. And I mean this!" Julie said, reaching down and grabbing a handful of off-white paint, throwing it at her sister. It landed all over Janine's shirt and partially in her curly hair. Janine's eyes widened, her mouth dropping open as she stared down at her shirt and then back up at her sister.

"Are you kidding me? Seriously? How old are you?" But before Julie could answer the question, Janine leaned down and grabbed her own handful of paint and smeared it down the front of Julie's T-shirt.

"Oh, you're asking for it now!" Julie said, as she grabbed another handful of paint and chased her sister, who was now running across the room.

The two women spent the next ten minutes grabbing handfuls of paint and smearing it all over each other. Occasionally they would smear it on the walls by accident, and it looked like some sort of off-white crime scene when they were finished. As she ran around like an immature middle schooler, Julie knew she should stop. But something was overtaking the logical part of her brain. She felt like a kid again, fighting with her older sister and trying to win at all costs.

"Oh my gosh. Look what we've done," Julie said as they

both stood on opposite sides of the room, out of breath and covered in paint. There literally wasn't one square inch of their bodies that wasn't now off-white. Julie could barely see through her eyes.

Janine looked around. "Dawson is going to kill us. Not only did we waste all of the paint, but the walls are messed up and the floor is atrocious."

Julie slid down to the floor against the wall, taking the inside of her shirt and wiping her eyes.

"I can't believe we did this. Here I was trying to save money and now he's probably going to have to refinish these floors and do something special with these walls."

Janine started laughing. "I guess you do need to get a job."

"Oh, you think this is funny? If you had any clue how to clean up a paint spill, we wouldn't be in this mess."

Janine sat down beside her. "You're not blaming this on me. You're the genius who decided to pour paint down a tiny tube without using a funnel."

"Well, you could've suggested that. You saw me doing it."

The two women sat there, backs against the wall for a few moments.

"Do you think there's any hope that we will ever get along?" Julie finally asked.

"I think so. We did when we were kids. Maybe you could come to counseling with me."

Julie laughed. "No. I don't have anything to talk about at counseling."

"I think you might. I mean, you've just gone through a terrible break up, so at least you might want to talk about that."

"No offense, but I have no interest in talking to a bunch of strangers about my problems. Working on this house will do plenty to get me back to my normal self."

"Is that what you want? Your normal self?"

"And just what is that supposed to mean?"

"I just mean are you happy as your normal self?"

"I thought I was. Even up until the moment Michael came home from that business trip and threw our lives into a tailspin, I thought we were happy. I thought I had everything I ever wanted. We were going to move to the beach and live out the rest of our lives riding bicycles along the shore and visiting the local coffee shop. I never expected that he would pull the rug out from under me."

"Look, I don't want to make you mad again. I think there might be another gallon of paint somewhere around here... But, I do think that maybe you wanted this vision of the perfect life. You wanted people to think everything was great. But for a long time, I didn't feel like you were the sister I knew. I felt like maybe you were settling in your life."

Julie knew she was right. But she sure wasn't going to admit it.

"I think I have about had it for tonight. Besides, I'm pretty sure Dawson is going to scream when he walks in here in the morning so that should wake us up. I think I'm going to take a shower and then hit the sack."

"Me too. It's been a long day."

The two women stood up and started turning off the lights and locking the doors. Julie didn't know why she even locked the doors. There was no one around, and everyone on the island had been there for ages. It wasn't like it was going to be a high crime area, but she was used to having some semblance of home safety having lived in the suburbs.

"Hey, Julie?"

"Yeah?"

"I'm sorry we still don't really get along all that well."

"Me too."

"I mean, maybe you're right. Maybe this won't ever be the kind of relationship we wish we could have. But, at the very least, maybe we will be able to sit across from each other at the Christmas table this year. That would be progress, right?"

Julie thought for a moment. "Yes, that would be progress." She turned so Janine couldn't see the sadness on her face as they walked toward the bedroom. She wanted so much more from their relationship, but maybe it just wasn't meant to be.

CHAPTER 10

"*J* don't even know what to say," Dawson said as he stood there next to Janine and Julie. He slowly scanned the room, his big green eyes widening over and over. Julie truly felt like a child who was about to be scolded by a parent.

"We are so sorry, Dawson. We were trying to help you by painting this room…"

"Do me a favor, ladies. Don't ever try to help me again."

Janine giggled under her breath. "Sorry," she said, when she noticed Dawson looking at her, his face impassable.

Dawson leaned down and picked up one of the drop cloths that he'd left so neatly folded in the corner. He stared at it for a moment, shook his head and rolled it into a ball, tossing it into an empty orange bucket.

Janine looked at her sister, unsure of what to say. Julie nodded her head toward the front door, indicating to Janine that she needed to get the heck out of dodge for awhile. Janine slipped out, probably happy to get away.

Maybe he was truly angry, Julie thought, as she watched him start cleaning up their mess. She walked to the other side of the room, picking up a paint brush that she'd tossed at her sister's head.

"I really am so sorry, Dawson. Please don't clean this mess up. Let me do it."

He didn't make eye contact. "I appreciate the offer, but I need to stay on schedule, and painting is on my schedule today." He continued walking around, sometimes stopping to stare at the paint covered floor as if he was trying to figure out what to do.

Dawson pulled his phone from his pocket and sent a text. He then went back to work. Julie hated this feeling. The guy was basically a stranger to her, even though he was her best friend on the island. But, she still didn't like feeling like he was mad at her.

"I assume we'll need to sand the floors or something?" she finally asked.

"I texted my guy. He'll come take a look at them tomorrow... see what can be done."

Julie nodded, even though he wasn't looking at her, and turned back to clean up. She noticed him starting to tape the moldings, so she decided she could at least help him do that. When he put the tape down for a moment, she picked it up and pulled off a long string before he could stop her.

"Julie, you don't need to help me. This is my job."

"Let me help. Please. I feel just awful about all of this. And embarrassed."

He finally turned to look at her. "What happened exactly?"

She pressed the tape to the wall and turned back to him. "My sister and I happened. We're like oil and water, and we can trigger each other very easily. She said something, or maybe I said something first... I can't remember, honestly. Before I knew it, we were throwing handfuls of paint at each other."

He smiled slightly. "I bet that was quite a relief on the pressure valve that is your relationship, huh?"

"In the moment. Not so much when we finished and realized what we'd done. When we tried to clean up, it just made it worse. We just weren't thinking about how this might affect you, and I'm sorry for that. Again."

Dawson chuckled. "It's okay. Really. I was taken a little aback by it, for sure. But I understand sibling stuff. Next time, maybe take it outside?"

Julie nodded, relieved that he wasn't mad at her. "Will do." She peeled off another piece of tape and leaned down to place it against the molding. "Say, do you know a lady on the mainland named Dixie? She runs a bookstore."

"Of course. Everybody knows Dixie. She's hard to miss with that sky high hairdo and that loud voice of hers." He chuckled as he said it, a look of familiarity on his face.

"She told me about you and Trina Cox."

He stopped dead in his tracks and stared at the wall, his face turning a shade of crimson she'd hadn't seen before. "What?"

Julie giggled. "Did a little skinny-dipping, did ya?"

"We live at the ocean. Everyone has done a little skinny-dipping," he said, trying to play it off. "What else did she tell you?"

"Nothing, She was more or less talking about her life."

"And her sons?"

"Yes."

Dawson stopped working and leaned agains the wall. "Her youngest son died, ya know?"

"She told me."

"Dang near killed Dixie. But she's one strong woman, for sure."

"She also told me about William, her older son."

"Yeah, he's a piece of work. We were good friends when

we were coming up. He was a nice guy. Liked to fish and surf. But when his daddy got sick and Dixie followed Johnny's wishes, well, William lost his mind, I think. He was just so desperate to blame somebody for his daddy's death. Haven't seen him in years."

"Dixie hasn't either. She said he never responded to her letters. It's so sad. I can't imagine losing my girls like that."

Dawson turned back to his work, pulling off long pieces of tape and putting them on the wall just right. "Family can be a weird thing. Sometimes, they're all you've got. Other times, they can be your worst enemy."

They continued working and chatting about anything and everything. Julie was surprised at how easily they got along and how much they had in common. Same favorite color - the sky blue you can only see at the ocean. Same favorite animal - dogs, of course. Same favorite holiday - Christmas. Maybe not earth shattering, but it made her feel connected to someone, at least.

"Well, I'd better get to painting if I want to finish up today. I hope you don't mind me leaving around five?"

"No, of course not. More work around the inn tonight?"

Dawson looked uncomfortable. "Nah. I've actually got a date tonight."

Julie froze for a moment. Why did that idea bother her? She was in the middle of a divorce, and her heart was not nearly ready for new love. She wasn't sure she'd ever be ready.

~

"So, you actually like it there?" Colleen asked from the other end of the phone line.

"I do. I mean, it's not exactly what I pictured, but it's growing on me a bit."

"And this Dawson guy?"

"Have you been talking to your grandmother?" Julie asked, rolling her eyes so hard that Colleen could probably hear it across the miles.

"Maybe."

"Look, he's my contractor. And my new friend here on the island. But that's it."

"Mom, it's okay to be interested in someone. I mean, Dad..." she started to say, before stopping herself.

"Dad what? Cheated on me, got another woman pregnant and then proposed to her?"

There was a deafening silence. Julie wished she could take the words back. She never wanted to be that person who bad mouthed her ex to her children.

"Sorry. I shouldn't have said that."

"I get it, Mom. I'd be livid if I was you too. I honestly don't know how to feel about him myself right now. But, he's still my Dad..."

"Colleen, I know you love him. And you should. He's been a good father to you and Meg. And he was a good husband for a lot of years." She wanted to say "as far as I know" at the end, but she stopped herself.

"I just want you to know that Meg and I would never have a problem with you dating this guy... or any guy... as long as he was nice to you and treated you right."

Julie smiled. "Honey, I'm not ready to date anyone. I may never be."

"Don't say that. You're too young to be alone forever."

As Julie stared out at the cars passing on the street in front of Dixie's bookstore, she thought about the prospect of being alone. Celebrating holidays alone. Birthdays by herself. It was all too much to think about. But she also never wanted to choose a man just because she didn't want to be alone. How sad was that?

"Well, as I said, Dawson is my friend, And plus he went on a date last night, so he's not interested in me anyway."

Colleen giggled. "Sounds like a sore subject."

"Very funny. I've got to go because my other new friend, Dixie, is bringing me what appears to be the biggest cupcake I've ever seen. We'll talk soon, okay?" she said before hanging up.

Dixie was standing there holding what could only be described as a small cake. No cupcake was supposed to be that large. It was covered in thick, white icing.

"What on Earth?" Julie said. Dixie joined her at the small bistro table she'd added to the sidewalk in front of her store.

"A new vendor came by today and brought this sample. It's red velvet, and I thought I'd share it with ya," Dixie said, handing her a fork.

"This is a sample?"

"They make the world's largest cupcakes, he said. I personally think it's just a cake, but I wasn't gonna tell him that."

Julie chuckled. "So, how's business?"

"It's been picking up, but I keep having to close early," she said, taking a big bite of the white frosting.

"Close early? Why?"

"Well, my afternoon girl, Chelsea, went back to college in Charleston. And I just haven't had time to run an ad to replace her. This time of the summer is just so busy. This is the first lull I've had today."

"I guess that's a good thing, right?"

"I 'spose so, but I'm getting older, and I sure would like some time off. I never get to sit in the sun on the beach or volunteer to count the dolphins."

"Count the dolphins?"

"Yes. I love to volunteer with a local non-profit. We count the dolphins every year to help scientists learn more about their behavior and help with conservation. I've done it for years, but I haven't got to do it the last two years."

"That sounds so interesting."

"There's so much to do around these parts, and protecting our wildlife is important."

Julie made a mental note to check into opportunities to learn more about the local area and wildlife.

"Maybe I could help you, Dixie."

"What do you mean?"

"Well, I'm going to need a part-time job around here. Would you consider hiring me?"

A huge smile spread across Dixie's face. "Seriously? I'd love to have you working here!"

"I have to admit I've never worked at a bookstore before, but I think I could learn."

Dixie reached across and patted her hand. "I know you'd do great. Let me go get the paperwork, and we'll get you working sooner rather than later! I'm just so excited!" she said as she walked back inside. Julie laughed and then took a bite of the cupcake, its ropey sweetness almost overwhelming. But it was far too good not to take a second bite.

"Is this what they call emotional eating?"

She looked up to see Dawson standing there, the sun shining behind him. He looked like an angel that had come to Earth to judge her poor eating habits.

"Oh, hey. You scared me."

"Sorry," he said, sliding down into the chair across from her. His big frame was so much more pronounced sitting in the small wrought iron chair.

"No biggie. Dixie wanted me to try this cupcake."

"That's a cupcake? Looks more like a small wedding cake." He reached over and scooped up a stray mound of icing before licking it off the end of his finger. Wow. That was more entertaining than she would have imagined.

"Well, all I know is it's good," Julie said. He looked at her for a long moment, a crooked smile slowly appearing on his face. "What?"

"You have a little icing right there…" he said, first pointing and then just reaching across and brushing it off the edge of her mouth with his thumb. Dear Lord, it had been such a long time since a man had touched her face like that. He was her friend. He was her friend. She just kept repeating the phrase in her mind.

"Thanks," she said, trying not to let him hear her voice tremble. Thankfully, Dixie came bursting back out of the bookstore in her usual; flamboyant way, taking the awkwardness out of the situation in the process.

"Here ya go, dear. Just some silly paperwork, and then we'll be co-workers! Oh, hi there, Dawson," she said, finally noticing someone was in her chair.

Dawson stood and kissed Dixie on the cheek. "Hey, pretty lady. What's this about being co-workers?"

Dixie grinned and put her arm around Dawson's waist, his body towering over hers like a large tree. "Well, Julie here has offered to come work here so I can get some time off. Isn't that grand?"

He smiled down at her and then looked at Julie. "That's wonderful. I'm sure you'll love working with this great lady."

"Aw, he's always been the sweetest," she said, hugging him closer. "You know, you've been like a son to me."

"It's my honor," he said, kissing the top of her head.

Julie wanted to melt into a puddle right there. He was perfect. There was no getting around it. He was astonishingly handsome, extremely talented, kind hearted, smelled like heaven…

"Julie?" Dawson said, waving his hand in front of her. She snapped back to reality and noticed Dixie was back inside the bookstore waiting on a customer and Dawson was sitting again. How long had she been daydreaming?

"Yeah?"

"You seemed lost in thought there for a minute."

"Sorry. I've got a lot going through my head. So, what are you doing on the mainland?"

"I needed some different nails for some of the porch boards, and a few other things. The tile guy is coming tomorrow morning, so your new bathrooms will be done soon."

"I cannot wait."

"They're installing the garden tub now, and my buddy, Dan, is putting in a new sink in the kitchen."

"It's really coming together, isn't it?" she said, unable to hide her smile.

"It is. I'm so happy for you, Julie. You deserve a fresh start."

"Thanks. So, how'd your date go last night?" It was a personal question. She shouldn't have asked. She knew that in her heart, but she wanted to know, if for no other reason than to live vicariously through someone else who was dating. But the look on his face made her sorry she asked.

"Not great."

"Oh, really? Sorry."

"Yeah, I wasn't expecting much. It was a set up by a friend of a friend. She's more of a city woman, if you know what I mean."

"Dawson, I'm from the city," Julie said, laughing.

"Yeah, but you're not a city woman."

"How do you figure?"

"I don't know how to explain it. But you're... deeper."

"You think so?"

"I do."

"So what went wrong on your date?" she asked, trying to sound nonchalant as she took another bite of the cupcake.

"Well, for one thing, she can't swim."

"And she lives near the beach?" Julie was incredulous.

"Right? Crazy. Anyway, she also hates being outside. We sat at an outdoor restaurant, and she complained nonstop about the heat."

"Why did your friend fix you up with this person?"

"Who knows?" he said, laughing. "But, I'm not making wedding plans anytime soon."

"Do you want to get married one day?"

"I was married for a time, back in my twenties, actually."

"Really? Mind if I ask what happened?"

He paused for a moment. "She passed away."

Julie froze, her fork in mid air. "I'm so sorry I asked, Dawson. It wasn't my place."

"You're my friend, Julie," he said, a soft smile on his face. "You can ask me anything."

"I'm so sorry for your loss."

"Her name was Tania. We met on a deep sea fishing trip that was set up in my senior year of high school. We got married two years later. We were married for five years, planning our future, when she told me she was pregnant. We were over the moon excited."

"You have a child then?"

His face fell a bit as he stared into the distance behind her, memories obviously overloading his brain.

"No. When she was six months along, she went into labor early. They tried to stop it, but the baby came and didn't survive. It was a boy. We named him Gavin. He was so cute. Had a head full of dark brown hair, just like I did when I was born. The men in my family are blessed with great hair," he said, a small smile on his face.

"I'm so sorry about Gavin. That must've been devastating," she said, holding back tears.

"It was. It still is when I really think about it. I'll sometimes think of what he'd be doing now, ya know? Maybe he'd be working with me renovating your house, learning carpentry."

"I'm sure Tania was shattered when she lost her son too."

His eyes welled with tears, and he wiped a stray one that escaped, before clearing his throat. "She never knew."

"What?"

"She started bleeding. They couldn't stop it in time."

"Oh my gosh..." Julie reached out and put her hand over his.

"There was nothing I could do. I just stood there, helpless, watching the nurses hover over my baby on one side of the room and my wife on the other. Then, they ushered me out as all of these people came running in to try to help her. A few minutes later, they came out and told me she was gone. Her mother passed out. It was terrible. Worst day of my life."

Julie didn't know what to say. Her own problems seemed trivial in comparison now. How had this man survived all of this?

"I'm in awe of you," she said without thinking.

"What?"

"You've just been through so much loss. Your wife, your child, your brother. How have you managed to come out the other side being such a kind, caring man? I think I'd be in the fetal position. I'd hate God and everyone around me."

He smiled. "I don't hate God. I sometimes don't understand why I've lost the people I love, but then I see the beauty of the marsh and the ocean, and I know there's a bigger purpose, ya know?"

"I wish I did. I'm angry, and my problems are so much

smaller than yours. I feel awful having even complained about them to you."

"Julie, your grief over losing your marriage is no less important than my grief. Loss is loss. But I hope that experiencing Seagrove fully will really help you see that there's more in this life for you. And for me."

"I hope so too."

CHAPTER 11

*J*ulie stood behind the cash register and waited for her first customer of the day. Working at Down Yonder had been interesting to say the least. Dixie had trained her over the course of a week, and the two of them had had more fun than should've been allowed at work. They'd blared music when customers weren't in the store, pigged out on cupcakes and cookies and gossiped about all of the new people Julie was meeting in town.

But, today seemed slower. The summer was winding down a bit as more schools started in other areas. Tourists were more interested in being at the beaches and local restaurants than coming to the little mom and pop bookstore.

She decided to busy herself straightening one of the bookshelves. Then, she heard the bell on the door and walked to the front. Dawson was standing there, a bag in his hand.

"Hey there!" Julie said, always happy to see her friend. Of course, she saw him almost everyday at home as he was always working on something. Her house was more livable now, and it was almost time to start the decorating process.

"Hey. Boy, this place is empty today."

"Yeah, I'm pretty bored. What's in the bag?"

"Old Mr. Schuster isn't feeling well, so I offered to pick up his prescription. He's the man who lives in the little green house by the bridge."

"Ah, yes, I know the one. That was nice of you to pick it up for him."

"No big deal. Where's Dixie today?"

"She's at a training for something about protecting sea turtles. All I know is she was very excited to get back to volunteering more," Julie said as she went back behind the counter and leaned against it.

Someone walked into the store, interrupting their conversation. It was a middle aged man wearing a suit, not something they commonly saw around town. Everybody wore shorts and flip flops, even on the mainland.

"Can I help you?" Julie asked.

The man walked to the counter and sat his briefcase there. "I'm looking for Julie Pike."

"Oh. That's me."

He popped open the briefcase and pulled out a folder. "Then I guess you've been served." He handed her the folder, closed his briefcase and walked out.

Julie stood there, stunned, holding the folder. "What on Earth?"

"Sounds like someone sent you legal papers?"

She opened the folder and saw the word divorce at the top. Then it made more sense.

"My divorce papers," she said, softly. It wasn't like she wasn't expecting them. But Michael had texted to tell her they could handle this amicably and not get attorneys involved. Looked like he changed his mind.

"I'm sorry."

"I mean, I knew I would get them eventually," she said, looking them over. "But it's obvious that Michael wanted everything done by the book to protect his money."

"Can't you get alimony?"

She closed the folder and sighed. "Maybe. But I don't want it, honestly. I want a fresh start, and I don't even want his money near me. Probably sounds stupid and short sighted to you."

Dawson shook his head. "No, actually it sounds strong. Listen, I want to show you something. What time do you get off?"

"We close at three today."

"Okay. I'm going to draw a little map here," he said as he sketched out the shape of the island. "Meet me here at four," he said, as he placed a big X on the paper.

"What is that?"

"You'll see," he said, smiling. "Don't be late!"

He walked out of the door, waving as he went, and Julie wondered what was in store for her.

~

WAS THIS A DATE? This couldn't be a date. They were friends, nothing more. And she wasn't even officially divorced yet. These were the thoughts Julie was thinking as she drove over the bridge and back onto Seagrove.

Did he like her as more than a friend? Did she feel the same way? Was this too soon? Did she even know the signs of someone liking her?

She looked down at the little map Dawson had drawn and then looked at the time on her car clock. A late customer had kept her at Down Yonder longer than expected, and now she was rushing to meet him in time. She would have preferred to go home first, change her clothes and make herself more presentable.

This is not a date, she reminded herself.

She pulled down a small road that she honestly hadn't noticed before and parked where Dawson put the X. His truck was sitting there, so at least she knew she was in the right place.

She stepped out of her car and looked around. "Dawson?" she called, a bit of a quiver to her voice. This was how those real crime shows started on TV.

"Over here!" Dawson called from down a path to her right. She followed his voice and then stopped.

"Where are you?"

"Look up," he said. She craned her head and saw the silhouette of him above her in a tree with thick, low hanging branches covered in moss.

"What are you doing up there, crazy person?" she yelled back.

He climbed down and jumped the last few feet, landing in front of her. "The better question is what are you doing down here?"

"If you think I'm climbing up into this tree, you've lost your mind," she said, turning to walk back to her car.

"I guess your sister *is* the more adventurous one."

She stopped in her tracks and turned around. "Excuse me?"

"I bet she'd climb this tree." He stood there, his face expressionless.

"Are you trying to be mean?"

"I'm trying to show you the island from a different perspective."

"I don't like heights, Dawson."

"Do you like staying in your box?"

"You're being awful right now."

He finally smiled. "I was trying to be a tough guy. I can see that doesn't work well with you."

"No, it doesn't," she said, rolling her eyes. "Seriously, I hate heights."

"I would never let you fall. I hope you know that."

She sighed. "I believe you. But, I can see everything just fine down here on the safe ground."

"Not what I'm going to show you."

He was peaking her interest, but not enough to cause her to risk life and literal limb.

Dawson walked closer. "Your husband is a freaking jerk."

"Tell me something I don't know," she said with a laugh. Dawson stood right in front of her.

"He's in Boston right now with some tart while you're here starting over."

"You're being mean again."

"He thinks you need him. He thinks he got to you. He thinks you'll always stay in your little box and not have a life without him."

"Oh, I see what you're doing now. You're trying to goad me into climbing this tree to spite my husband."

Dawson pointed upward. "This tree represents you climbing out of that pit of marriage you were in... all those lies... all that betrayal. And when you get to the top, you'll see your whole new beautiful future laid out in front of you. Don't you want to see that? Don't you want to push past all of your fears? Don't you want to be something... someone... totally new?"

It was working. He was getting to her.

Julie took in a deep breath and blew it out. "Yes! I want to climb up there! But if you let me fall, I will haunt you forever."

Dawson laughed. "I believe it."

Slowly but surely, he helped her climb up the lower

branches. Every time she faltered, he was there with a steady hand on her back, pushing her upward. The man was strong, no doubt about it. She tried not to think of whether he was looking at her butt. After all, she'd had two kids and no gym membership for a few months.

Every so often, they'd stop for a moment to catch their breaths, but Julie didn't dare look down. She was afraid she might just pass out if she did.

"Just reach up and grab that platform," Dawson said, as they neared the top. Sure enough, she felt around and there was a flat area made with two by fours. He pushed her up a bit and she crawled onto the area, never so happy to be anywhere in her life. The thought of having to get back down was a bit terrifying, though.

Dawson joined her a few moments later. They didn't speak for a moment as they caught their breaths again, but then Julie finally looked outward and saw the most beautiful view she'd ever seen.

"Oh my goodness. Look at this!" she said, not thinking about the fact that he'd probably seen it a million times in his life. "Why is this platform here?"

"This property belonged to my uncle when I was a kid. We built this together so we could see the best views of the island."

"It's gorgeous, Dawson. I mean, I can see the whole stretch of beach over there and then the views of the marsh over here." She stared at it for a few moments before looking at him. "Thanks for making me do this."

"Glad you like it," he said with a wink. Between that and the crooked smile, she felt like she needed to fan herself.

Julie pulled her phone out of her pocket and pressed the camera app.

"What are you doing?" he asked, reaching over and touching her phone.

"I was going to take pictures of these beautiful views."

"You can't do that."

Julie was confused. "Why?"

"Because a picture can't capture this present moment. It can't capture the smell or the sounds or the colors. You have to save those in your mind."

"You're pretty deep yourself, Dawson Lancaster," she said, sliding her phone back into her pocket.

"This place is beyond what you can express in a photo," he continued as he looked out over the marsh. "People can't understand why I love it here so much, but once you see the island from up here, it's hard to ever leave."

She looked around again, closed her eyes and took in a deep breath. It really was the most tranquil place on Earth. In all of her visualizations about a beach house, this wasn't what she'd pictured. Instead, she'd always seen the requisite glass front beach house sitting on white sand with multiple decks overlooking the ocean.

But this was somehow better. It was real. It was beautiful and complicated and simple at the same time.

"I'd like to teach you some things about this area, if you want to learn?"

"Of course! I'm all ears."

"Okay. This tree we're sitting in is called a live oak. These are the ones covered in moss that line the streets on the mainland. They're great for climbing, as you can see."

"Yes, I can definitely attest to that," she said, smiling.

"We also have other trees like the black gum, longleaf pine and river birch. The river birch trees are the ones that look like the bark is peeling off. See, there's one over there." He pointed off into the distance as Julie followed along.

"I think I have one in my yard. I thought it was dying."

"Nope. That's just how they look."

"Glad I didn't cut it down," she said.

"This area has over three-hundred fifty thousand acres of everything from beaches to saltwater marshes to cypress swamps. We've got several endangered species here including loggerhead turtles and bald eagles. Of course, we have our share of alligators here too."

"Terrifying."

"Generally speaking, if you leave them alone, they'll leave you alone."

"I'll keep that in mind. So, tell me, in the marsh, what is all that grass called?"

"Cord grass."

"Man, you're a wealth of information."

He smiled. "Growing up here, we learned a lot about our own area in school. We take pride in this coastal area and all of the unique parts of it. From the plants to the bugs, I spent my whole childhood learning everything I could. I wanted to be a biologist."

"Why didn't you become one?"

"Aw, life got in the way, I suppose. But I still get to learn as much as I want. I just don't get paid for it. Now, you've noticed the tide comes in and out of the marsh behind your place, right?"

For the next hour, Dawson explained just about every part of the island and surrounding areas. He was like her own personal tour guide, giving her fact after fact. She worried there might be a test later.

As she watched him, she was in awe yet again. His knowledge, and excitement about his home, was fun to watch. She'd never felt close to her hometown where she grew up. But Seagrove was already starting to feel like home and like a place she could never imagine leaving.

"Thanks for bringing me up here," Julie said after they'd finished talking.

"You're very welcome. Sorry I talked so much."

"I'm not. It was nice to hear about this new place I call home."

He smiled. "Do you think you'll stay here?"

She nodded. "I actually think I will."

"Good."

"I'd better get going. I promised Janine I'd make the sandwiches tonight. I'll be so glad to get my new oven!"

"Say, why don't you ladies come to my place tonight? Lucy is cooking shrimp and grits tonight, and of course her famous peach cobbler. There will be plenty for all of us, trust me."

Julie thought for a moment. "Are you sure?"

"Absolutely! Just don't bring any paint with you, okay?"

"Very funny," she said, as they started to climb down out of the tree.

$\sim$

"Janine? Are you home?"

Julie walked around the house, calling her sister's name. She walked down the hall, but didn't see her. Finally, she spotted her standing out back near the marsh, her cell phone to her ear.

"Oh, hey. I didn't realize you were home. I was talking to Mom. Be glad you didn't get home in time to talk to her too."

"Yeah, I just got here. I don't think I could take a call with Mom today. Might ruin my good mood."

"Well, it certainly ruined mine," Janine said, laughing, as she walked over and grabbed a bottle of water.

"So, Dawson has invited us to dinner at his place tonight."

Janine turned around and did a kissy face. "Oh, Dawson…"

"Stop. It's not like that. He's my friend. Jeez, why does everyone do this? It's so immature."

"Because he's a hunk, first off. And secondly, he's here *all* the time."

"He's renovating my house!"

"Whatever. What's that?" she asked, pointing at the folder in Julie's hand.

"Divorce papers. Michael had me served at the bookstore today."

"Are you serious? That jerk. I thought he said…"

"He did. But, as is customary with him, it was apparently a big, fat lie."

"What do the papers say?"

"I haven't even read them, honestly. We've already sold the house and our kids are grown, so I don't know why he went to the trouble of hiring an attorney. There's nothing left to negotiate since I'm not asking for alimony."

Janine reached her hand out for the papers. "Can I see?"

"Are you an attorney now?" Julie asked, handing her the folder.

"No, but I watch a lot of court TV shows now that I'm unemployed, so that basically makes me one."

Janine looked through the papers, and then her eyes widened.

"What?"

"Were you aware that Michael owns a condo in Boston?"

Julie snatched the papers back. "What? Are you kidding me?" She searched the lines of text until she found the information. Michael had purchased the place ten months before they broke up.

"He never told you?"

"Of course not!"

"You have to fight him for half of that money, Julie."

"I don't want to keep dragging this out, Janine. I just want it to be done and over with," she said, tossing the file across the kitchen counter.

"You deserve that money. He used your marital finances to buy it. And you deserve alimony too!"

"I don't want alimony."

"Okay, fine. But you need to fight for that condo money. It's the right thing to do."

"I'll think about it."

"Good. I'd better go take a shower before we go to Dawson's. I want to make a good impression on my future brother in law," she said, as she quickly ran down the hallway.

"Not funny!"

~

As THEY STOOD on Dawson's front porch, Julie thought about Michael's latest lie. How could he take their marital funds and buy himself a condo so he could be close to his floozy? Yes, floozy. She still used that word even if it was old timey.

"Good evening, ladies!" Dawson said, as he answered the door. The smell of his cologne draped over Julie like a warm blanket, mixed with the saltwater scent of the ocean behind his house. All of her favorite things rolled into one.

"Thanks for inviting us, especially after our little paint escapade," Janine said.

"Let's not talk about that," Dawson said with a laugh as he opened the door to allow them inside.

He introduced Lucy to Janine as they all sat down at the table. On the table was quite a spread of Lowcountry dishes including finger sandwiches with pimento cheese, pickled okra, shrimp and grits and fried oysters.

"I hope you ladies are hungry. Lucy has cooked up quite a feast here," Dawson said.

"I'm starving, but Lucy, I hope you'll join us too?" Julie asked.

"Oh, sugar, I already ate my fair share while I was cooking. Besides, my grandson has a band concert on the mainland tonight, so I'm going to say my goodbyes now."

"Goodnight, Lucy. Have fun at the concert!" Julie said.

After Lucy left, Dawson surveyed the table. "Dang. Lucy forgot to bring out the Hoppin' John."

"Hoppin' John? What is that?" Janine asked.

"It's a staple in these parts. Basically, it's a dish with peas and rice, of course we season it up. We eat it on New Year's Day, but we try to have it a few times during the year too. Let me go grab that from the kitchen."

Dawson got up and walked back to the kitchen. "I feel like I stepped into some kind of Southern novel," Janine said.

"I feel right at home," Julie said.

"I can see that," Janine replied, a sly smile on her face.

"Okay, here we go. Hoppin' John is on the table. We're now ready to dig in."

"I can't wait!" Janine said, leaning over to scoop food onto her plate.

"Who'd like to say grace?" Dawson asked. Janine slowly dropped the serving spoon and sat upright.

"Sorry."

"No problem. Around here, we like to thank God for our blessings. I know it's old fashioned for some, but it has served me well."

Julie smiled. "Why don't you do the honor?"

Dawson nodded and closed his eyes. Janine and Julie followed suit.

"Dear Heavenly Father, thank you for this food and these friends who will share it with me. I'm so grateful for the blessings in my life, including these new friends and this beautiful island I call home. Bless this food for the nourishment of our bodies. Amen."

"That was lovely, Dawson," Julie said.

"So, how's the job going at the bookstore? Do you like working with Dixie?"

"Yes, I love it. She's such a character. Reminds me a little bit of this one right here," Julie said, cutting her eyes at her sister.

"Oh really? And you love her?"

"Very funny."

"How does she remind you of me?"

Julie took a bite of the Hoppin' John and fell immediately in love with it. That was something she'd definitely be making when her kitchen was ready.

"Well, she's eccentric, for one thing. Marches to the beat of her own drummer."

"And you like those qualities in her, but you don't like them in me?"

"Janine, let's not go down this rabbit hole. We're trying to have a nice dinner here."

"I think she has a valid question," Dawson said, trying to contain his smile as he looked down at his food.

"Oh really?" she said, struggling not to kick him under the table. They didn't know each other quite well enough for that yet.

"Thank you, Dawson. So? How do you love those qualities in her and not me, sis?"

"It's not that I don't love your eccentricities and quirks, Janine. It's that you tried to pass them along to my completely normal daughters."

Janine stopped eating and looked at her. "So I'm not normal?"

"Do you think you are?"

The two women stared at each other for a moment. "I don't want to be normal. I want to be me and have my own family love me for who I am and not try to change me. That's what I want."

Things were getting awfully heavy for dinner at a friend's house. "We do love you, Janine. We just don't always understand you."

"Well, I don't understand why you married a jerk and stayed with him for twenty years, but I don't harp on it all the time."

"I'm wondering why I did that myself."

Dawson chuckled. "Sorry. I didn't know I was opening a can of worms. Let's try a more neutral topic. How did you like your tree climb today?"

"*You* climbed a tree?" Janine said, looking at Julie with her eyes wide.

"Is that so surprising?"

"Well, given that you hate heights and bugs, I would say that, yes, it's surprising."

"I sort of tricked her into it."

"You goaded me into it."

"And why were you climbing trees?"

"I wanted to show her the island in a way other people don't get to see it. I'd be glad to take you up too."

Julie felt a sudden sense of jealousy she wasn't expecting, like tree climbing was what she and Dawson did together and no one else could do it. She shook her head a bit, trying to get the feeling out, but it wasn't in her head. It was in the pit of her stomach.

"I might take you up on that. I love climbing trees. I did some conservation work in California a few years ago and got to do a climb into a redwood tree."

"Wow! Those things can be massive. I'd love to see one up close one day."

The conversation went on for ten minutes, and Julie felt like a third wheel. Of course, Dawson would find Janine interesting because she was. As much as she hated to admit it to herself, being around Janine had always made her feel boring and inferior. Janine was girl-next-door beautiful with her perfect complexion and bouncy curls that hung to her shoulders. The longer she lived with her, the more she was starting to look like her old self again.

Julie was happy to see her depression lifting and her eating habits returning to normal after a few weeks of therapy sessions. But, she was also starting to feel those old jealous feelings again, and that just made her feel bad about herself.

When dinner was over, they thanked Dawson and got back into the car for the very short drive home.

"He's a nice guy. I see why you like him," Janine said as they drove.

"I don't like him like that."

Janine just chuckled and looked out the window.

CHAPTER 12

*J*ulie wiped down the bistro table and picked up two books someone had left. One was a book about South Carolina history, and the other was a women's fiction book about a dysfunctional family in the lowcountry. She read the back cover and smiled, remembering her childhood dreams of becoming a famous author. She rarely thought about that anymore, figuring she was too old to pursue silly dreams like that.

"Good afternoon, kid," Dixie said as she walked through the front door. "Whatcha got there?"

"Oh, just cleaning up some books a lady left on the table."

Dixie reached out and took the fiction book from her. "This one is written by Sadie Clark. She was a firecracker."

"Was?"

"She passed last year at the ripe old age of one hundred." Dixie handed the book back to Julie and then walked behind the counter and opened the cash register to check the change.

"Wow. When did she start writing books?"

"She was almost seventy when she wrote her first one. Had so many best sellers I can't even count."

"Seventy?"

Dixie smiled. "Sugar, you're never too old to follow your dreams. Seventy may seem old now, but it sure ain't when you're closing in on it like I am!"

"Oh, I didn't mean any disrespect. It's just that I've had this lifelong dream of becoming an author myself. Hearing about Sadie makes me wonder if I could do it."

"Well, of course you could do it! Listen, if there's one thing I've learned in all my years on this planet, it's that you need to pursue your dreams while you can. My late husband, Johnny, always had this dream of having a farm. He wanted to raise horses and cows and chickens. We had the money, but he just kept putting it off until we found out about his cancer. And then we couldn't do it. I could see the sadness in his eyes when he talked about how he had been too scared to follow his dreams and now it was too late." Dixie's eyes misted as she told the story.

"You've given me something to think about. This is a new beginning, after all. Maybe I should try my hand at writing my first book."

"Well, you surely have lots of inspiration around here!" Dixie said with a laugh.

"That is very true. Well, if you've got everything handled, I think I'm going to head home. I am very tired, and I think they finished up my kitchen today so I'm super excited to see it."

"You go on home. I've got it from here. See you tomorrow!" Dixie said as she walked away to welcome a new customer into the store.

~

Julie drove up to her house with excitement. She couldn't wait to see how the kitchen had turned out. Dawson was supposed to have workers there all day doing the countertops and new cabinets. She couldn't wait to cook her first meal in her brand new kitchen.

As she walked in the door, she was surprised to see her mother standing there talking to Dawson and Janine in the living room.

"Mom?"

"Hey, honey!" her mother said, as if it was the most natural thing in the world that she was standing there.

"I didn't know you were coming," she said as she hesitantly hugged her. "Did you know?" she mouthed to Janine from over her mother's shoulder. Janine shook her head and shrugged her shoulders.

"I decided to surprise you girls. So, how are things going with you two?" SuAnn looked at them expectantly, like leaving them alone for a few weeks was going to solve all of their problems.

The truth was, things were better than Julie had feared at the beginning. Not perfect, but better. They were getting along for the most part, but there were still moments that Julie was reminded of why she had broken ties in the first place.

"They're good, Mom," Janine said, obviously trying to ease her mother's mind.

"Well, I have to say your fella here has done a marvelous job with the cottage so far."

Dawson's eyes widened. "Mom. Dawson is my contractor, not my 'fella'." She mouthed sorry to Dawson. He smiled.

"Well, whatever the case. Anyway, it looks adorable." She continued looking around. "Will you be getting furniture, dear?"

Julie sighed. "Of course, Mother. Why would I live without furniture?"

"Well, it has been a few weeks. Do you have a bed to sleep on?"

"We sleep on air mattresses," Janine said. Julie could've strangled her.

"Air mattresses? Like blow up beds? Oh, no. That simply won't do. Let me take you shopping for some new furniture. My treat!"

The last thing Julie wanted to do was shop with her mother. Some of the worst experiences of her life involved shopping with her mother. Not only did she rush from store to store, making it hard for anyone to keep up with her little legs, but she was highly critical of everything Julie picked out. Plus, she liked to "people watch" as she called it, but it mostly consisted of SuAnn criticizing the way other people looked.

"She shouldn't be wearing those pants. Looks like they're five sizes too small."

"Good Lord, did you see her hair? The seventies called and want their hairstyle back."

It was all too much for Julie to take. Still, she did need furniture, and her mother had a good bit of money. If she was offering, it was hard to say no. Her budget, even with her part-time job at the bookstore, was running thin.

"Sure. We can drive over to Charleston and do some shopping if you'd like?" Julie said. Janine looked shocked. "Do you want to come too, Janine?"

"Um…"

"Of course, she does! She would never bow out of a shopping trip when her mother drove hours to see her. Right, Janine?"

Boy, her mother was a master manipulator.

"Right. Let me just freshen up a bit." Janine excused herself.

"I'm going to wait in the car. It's a bit warm in here, even for late September." She fanned herself as she walked outside, looking around like something might attack her between the house and the car.

"Sorry. She's just... well, there are no words."

"No apologies necessary. I see where Janine gets her eccentricity from."

Julie laughed. "I've never thought about it that way, but you're probably right."

"Did you see the kitchen?"

"Oh, wow, I totally forgot!" Julie walked around the corner and saw the most beautiful kitchen she'd ever seen. With sparkling beige marble countertops and rich wood cabinets, it was the perfect complement to her marsh land property.

"Dawson, it's gorgeous! And look at these tile floors, and the oven is amazing! You've done such an awesome job. It's really coming together!" Without thinking, Julie turned and hugged him tightly. He slipped his arms around her, pulling her close.

For a moment, time seemed to stand still. His hug felt like a warm blanket wrapped around her, and she felt truly safe for the first time in a long time. She didn't want to let go, but thankfully Dawson did.

"Sorry. I didn't mean to..."

"Julie, we're Southerners. We hug around here. It's okay." He smiled that lazy smile, and she honestly thought about asking for another hug. Thankfully, Janine re-appeared.

"Let's go get this over with. Does anyone have Xanax?"

"Not funny," Julie said as they walked toward the door.

"Who said I was joking?"

~

As PREDICTED, shopping with her mother had been challenging. Everything she liked, SuAnn said was "dreadful" or "white trash". Finally, the three women decided to head back to town and see what they could find locally.

As they passed Down Yonder, SuAnn laughed. "Good Lord, who names their bookstore something trite like that? It's embarrassing that other people around the country think Southerners are a bunch of buffoons saying 'yonder'."

"Pardon me?"

Julie hadn't realized that Dixie was watering the plants in front of the bookstore, down on her knees.

"Oh no. Mother, honestly, you need to think about what you say sometimes!" Julie said. "I'm so sorry, Dixie. This is my mother, SuAnn Lewis."

Dixie eyed her up and down. "Ah, your mother. That explains it."

It was obvious the two women were not fans of each other in that moment. SuAnn and Dixie couldn't have been any different if they tried.

"Pleasure to meet you, Dixie? Now, that's a Southern name if I've ever heard one."

Dixie smiled, but it wasn't her normal smile. It was the smile of a pissed off Southern lady who would wring your neck if she didn't think the police would drag her off to the pokey.

"I'm very proud of my Southern roots, SuAnn. And I do believe you were born in the South as well?"

"I was. But I always try to rise above my raising, as my momma used to say. And no offense intended on my comments about your adorable little bookstore's name."

"Honey, to be offended by your comments, I'd have to

care about them in the first place," Dixie said, the same sweet smile plastered on her face.

Janine was grinning from ear to ear like she wanted a bag of popcorn for the show.

"Well, let's be on our way, Mom. We have lots of shopping to do," she said, pushing her mother forward down the sidewalk. "I'm so sorry, Dixie," she whispered as they passed.

Dixie nodded and waved. "Don't you worry, sweetie. I know how to handle a woman like her."

Janine continued ushering their mother forward as Julie hung back for an extra moment. "Well, can you tell me how to handle her then?" Dixie laughed.

～

THEIR FINAL STOP was a small furniture store just before the bridge. Julie was planning to just let her mother criticize everything, go home and then she could choose her own furniture after she left. Of course, she'd have to pay for it, which would stink but would be entirely worth it to get what she wanted.

"Now, this is surprisingly lovely," SuAnn said, pointing at an off white sofa. She was actually spot on as the couch was exactly in line with the period the home was built. "And the price is reasonable. That's the good thing about shopping in poor areas."

"Mother, this isn't a poor area. You do realize the houses on the beach are in the millions, right?" Janine finally said.

"That seems like a rip off for the area. Anyhow, I think this sofa would fit nicely in the living room. What do you think, Julie?"

"Oh, do I get an opinion?"

"Of course you do, darling. I'm just here to help!"

"Right. Well, I actually do like it. And I think that blue chair over there would accent it nicely."

"Hey, Julie, did you see these tables over here?" Janine asked.

Within an hour, they'd picked out everything Julie needed for her living room, dining room and bedrooms. Her mother paid for all of it, thankfully, and it would be delivered the next day.

"Thank you for the furniture, Mom. I really do appreciate it," Julie said as they stood in front of her house, telling her mother goodbye before she made the trip back to the Georgia mountains.

"Just think of it as my contribution to your new start. Just knowing you girls are getting along makes my heart smile."

As bad as she could be, Julie knew she meant it. And if her health issue was serious, she wanted to give her mother this last wish of having her daughters together at the holidays.

"Have a safe trip," Janine said, trying to usher her mother along. She gave her a quick hug and then walked up to the porch.

"Say, how is Janine really doing?" SuAnn asked when she was out of earshot.

"Better, I think. She seems to really like it here."

"She looks a lot better, like she's gained some weight."

"She has. And she's going to a counseling group."

"Good. I know this has been hard, Julie Ann, but you're doing a good thing for her."

Finally, a normal conversation with her mother. She'd been waiting her whole life for this moment.

"And one day, you'll find a man again and won't have to live in this wild place."

Ah, there it was.

"Mom, this is my home. I don't ever plan to leave

Seagrove. I love my job and my friends and my house. I don't need a man to take care of me."

"Oh, Julie, I hope you'll change your mind one day."

"Have a safe trip, Mom."

SuAnn waved and got into her car, and Julie decided she was going to go eat a pint of ice cream.

~

"WHERE ARE WE GOING?" Janine asked as they continued to walk.

"I know it's around here somewhere. There's a big tree with moss covering it."

"Seriously," she said from behind. "All of the trees here are covered in moss, Julie!"

"Yeah, but this one is special. There's a platform… There it is!"

They walked closer and Janine looked up. "And Dawson built that?"

"Yes, when he was a kid. I'm telling you, it's the best view on the island."

"And you climbed it?"

"Yep. I was terrified, but it was so worth it. But, Dawson wouldn't let me take pictures of it because he said I needed to hold the image in my mind."

"He's a little woo woo sometimes."

Julie looked at her sister. "Really? And you're not?"

"Takes one to know one. So, why are we out here?"

"Well, for one thing, I want to show you the island and tell you some of the things I learned, like the fact that this here is a live oak tree."

"Okay…"

"And for the second thing, I'm writing a novel. Don't laugh!"

"Why would I laugh, Julie? I think that's awesome!"

Janine really did seem excited for her, and in that moment she felt guilty. Her sister was genuinely happy for her, and for so many years she'd just been flat out jealous of her good fortune.

"Really?"

"Of course! You've always been an amazing writer. I'm sure your novel will be great."

"Wow," Julie said, staring at her.

"What?"

"I thought you'd think it was silly."

"That makes me sad. We've gotten so off track through the years, haven't we?"

"We have."

Janine put her hands on Julie's shoulders. "I'm your big sister, and I'm always proud of you. And maybe I've been jealous of you from time to time. I'm sorry."

"Jealous of me? Why?"

"Because you had the life I wanted with a husband and kids and stability."

"You wanted that? But you traveled and never stayed in one place."

Janine shrugged her shoulders. "I was running from my feelings of inferiority."

"That sounds like shrink talk."

"Well, my therapist has helped me work through some things. What I've realized is that I was putting up a wall, trying to be different, as a way to get Mom's attention and not feel so envious of you."

Julie was stunned. "I was jealous of you all these years."

"Seriously?"

"Yes. I thought you judged me for having this boring life."

"I did, but it was just because you had what I wanted."

"Boy, we've really been messed up, huh?"

Janine giggled. "I guess so. But at least we figured it out, and we still have years ahead of us to be closer, right?"

"Right," Julie said, feeling like a weight was starting to lift off of her shoulders.

"So what does this large tree have to do with your novel?"

"I need to learn to describe this place better because my novel will be set here, on Seagrove Island. I want to get a good look, take some notes."

"We're going to climb it? Without Dawson?"

"We don't need a man, do we?" Julie asked, a grin on her face. "Besides, I don't want him to know I'm writing a book just yet."

"I guess we can try it," Janine said, uncertainty in her voice.

"Remember when we would climb the magnolia tree behind Uncle Dan's place in the mountains?"

"Yeah, but this is three times that size."

"True, but I think we can do it."

"Okay, then let's do it."

The two women took their time, carefully making their way to the platform. When Julie was finally sitting there, she took in a deep breath and sighed with relief.

"Look at this view!" She said.

Janine took it all in, her eyes wide. "Wow. It truly is beautiful. Look at the beach. I haven't been on that end before. I'll have to add it to my daily routine. I've started doing yoga on the beach, you know?"

"Really? You're doing yoga again, huh? Good for you."

"I thought you hated yoga and thought it was stupid?" Janine asked.

"Since the class you gave me, I have a whole new appreciation for it, trust me."

Janine laughed. "Thanks. That means a lot. I've been thinking about starting my own business."

"Really? Doing what?"

"Teaching yoga to trauma victims. My therapist said I could put a flyer in her office and probably have full classes. I was thinking of doing them on the beach."

"That's a great idea! I'm sure Dixie wouldn't mind if you put a flyer at the bookstore too."

"That would be great. I'm pretty excited about this new beginning."

"You know, you can stay with me as long as you want, Janine."

"Really? I don't want to overstay my welcome. I mean, we're doing well but I know there's still a lot of baggage between us."

Julie leaned her head over and put it on Janine's shoulder. "I think we can get through it."

"I do too," she said, leaning her head over too, as they watched the sea gulls dive bomb into the water in front of them.

After nearly falling out of the tree when they climbed down, Janine and Julie made it safely back to the cottage, famished from staying way too long in the tree.

Julie had taken meticulous notes and had lots of questions for Dixie, and maybe Dawson, about local vegetation. She wanted her book to be as realistic as possible.

"I'm going to take a nice, hot shower," Janine said as soon as they crossed the doorway. Dawson was standing in the kitchen, finishing up the tile backsplash Julie had added after the fact.

"Hey," he said. "Where'd you ladies run off to?"

She smiled. "We climbed the tree."

He stopped and turned around. "The tree? Alone?"

"Yes, we did," she said, proudly.

Dawson looked a little perturbed. "You could have fallen."

"What?"

"Ya'll shouldn't have been up there alone."

"No offense, Dawson, but we're grown women. We don't need a man to protect us."

He chuckled and shook his head. "Maybe not, but do you know there are ants in that tree that could send you to the hospital? Do you know which type of plants not to touch or you'll break out in a rash that'll make you want to die?"

"Well, no…"

"I'm not saying you need protection, but this island is unlike anywhere you've lived. You need to be safe."

"Sorry. I should've asked you. But, we're okay."

"Good," he said, finally smiling. "Did Janine like it?"

"Yes, she loved it. She's getting a shower."

Her phone rang, and she dug it out of her pocket.

"Hello?"

"Hi. I'm trying to reach Julie Pike."

"This is she."

"This is Nurse Linda Dunkin at Boston Regional Hospital. Is your husband Michael Aaron Pike?"

Her heart started racing. "Soon to be ex-husband, yes. Why?"

"He's been in a car accident, and it's pretty serious. You might want to come."

"But I live in South Carolina. Isn't his fiancee with him? Her name is Victoria."

"She has been here, yes. But you're still legally married, and you will need to make the decisions about his medical care."

She felt sick. As much as she hated Michael for what he'd done, she didn't wish him harm.

"Okay, I'll catch the next flight out."

She hung up the phone, her eyes overflowing with tears.

"What's going on?" Dawson asked. Janine walked down the hallway, a towel still wrapped around her.

"What's happening?" She asked.

"The hospital in Boston called. Michael was severely injured in a car accident. I'm still his wife, so they called me... I have to go..." she said, running around the room like a headless chicken.

"Julie, take a breath," Dawson said, holding onto her shoulders. She took in a couple of deep breaths and tried to calm down.

"Should I call the girls?" Janine asked.

"No. Not yet. I need to get there and see what's going on first. Where's the closest airport?"

"Charleston," Dawson said. "I'll drive you there."

"Okay."

"I'm going with you to Boston," Janine said.

"You don't have to."

Janine looked at her. "Yes, I do."

$\mathcal{A}$s Julie and Janine arrived at the hospital, Julie's heart was skipping and racing all over the place. She feared that she might need a hospital bed before it was over with. Her anxiety was at the highest level she could ever remember.

But, she was anxious about a whole bunch of things. What was Michael's condition? How would she tell her daughters? How would she interact with Victoria? How would she ever make life-and-death decisions for a man that she was so angry at? How could she be sure she was making the right decisions?

"Hi, my name is Julie Pike. Someone called me about my husband, Michael."

"Yes, we've been waiting for you to arrive. Let me get Dr. Sadler." The nurse walked away and made a phone call before returning to the desk. "Dr. Sadler will be with you shortly. You can wait right over there in that small room."

Julie and Janine walked over to the room and sat down.

"I can't believe how long it took me to get here. I would've just driven if I'd known I was going to have such a long wait to get a flight."

"You got here as soon as you could, Julie. This isn't your fault. And Dawson is holding down the fort at home. Dixie has the bookstore covered. You just need to concentrate on what you have to do here."

"I know. Thank you for coming with me."

"Of course. That's what sisters do, right?"

Julie reached over and held her sister's hand tightly. "I'm so glad we've been working on our relationship because, honestly, right now, I don't know what I would do without you."

"Well, you don't have to ever worry about that," she said as she put her arm around her sister and held her close.

A few moments later, Dr. Sadler appeared in the room. "Mrs. Pike?"

"That's me. And this is my sister, Janine."

"Nice to meet you. Why don't we go to my office so we can chat about Michael's condition." He waved them back out into the hallway. They followed him down a short distance and then went into a small office with just a desk and a couple of chairs.

"So, Michael was in a very serious automobile accident yesterday evening. When he first arrived in the emergency room, his condition was grave. He has a broken pelvis, a broken femur and multiple broken ribs. He has lacerations to his face, swelling around his eyes and a head injury that we don't yet know the extent of until he wakes up. We honestly weren't sure he was going to make it when I had my nurse call you."

"Oh my gosh. I just can't believe this is happening."

"I realize from my nurse's conversation with you that you and your husband are in the process of a divorce?"

"That's correct."

"And I'm sorry that we had to call you and have you travel here, but legalities being what they are…"

"No, it's fine. Michael and I were together for over twenty years, and we have two grown children together. They would expect me to take care of their dad and make sure he got proper medical care."

"Of course. I understand he is engaged to someone else?"

"Yes, that is also correct. And they have a child together."

Dr. Sadler looked at her and shook his head slightly before continuing. "So, I understand this might be something that causes conflicting emotions, having to take care of someone you have this kind of history with. But, honestly, to be candid, his fiancée doesn't seem very interested in being here to care for him."

Julie stared at him, like she wasn't understanding his words. She cocked her head to the side. "What?"

"To be frank, we have only seen her here once in the last twenty-four hours. She was here for about half an hour, just initially after he came in. When we asked her who she was, she seemed to distance herself. In fact, she told one of our nurses that she was not interested in caring for someone with such debilitating injuries."

"What a complete skanky narcissist!" Janine said, throwing her hands in the air. Julie held her hand up at her sister. "Janine, please. Dr. Sadler, what exactly are you saying?"

"I'm saying that you're his next of kin, even if it's just on paper. His condition is still very serious. He is not conscious right now and he has already had one surgery. We expect to do more surgeries in the coming days. He's going to require care here in the hospital for quite some time, and if his fiancee isn't interested in being here for him, we don't know who will sit with him and be his emotional support."

Julie realized what he was getting at. They wanted her to

stay, to play the doting wife until he was recovered. Life wasn't fair. Up until a few hours ago, she would've strangled him with her bare hands. Now she was expected to sit at the hospital and be his support system because his stupid fiancée wasn't interested in getting her hands dirty.

"What do you need me to do?"

"Well, the first thing would probably be to go see him. Although he can't respond, he might know that you're there. Sometimes our patients start to respond better when they hear a familiar voice. He's basically been alone in that room for twenty-four hours other than a short visit with his fiancée. And when she left, his blood pressure skyrocketed so we had to medicate him for that. Honestly, she may have said something to upset him. I don't know."

"Well, this is certainly a strange situation. But I'm here, and I will do what needs to be done. So yes, I'd like to see him. And then, if you can give me some more updates on his condition and prognosis, I would like to call my daughters and let them know. One is in California and the other is overseas at school."

"Certainly. Let me show you to his room, and then we can meet later."

Janine and Julie stood up, shooting each other glances, as they followed the doctor down the hall toward Michael's room.

~

THE NEXT FEW minutes were a blur. Janine stayed behind in a waiting room closer to Michael's room as Julie went inside. She couldn't believe what she saw. There were tubes and IVs everywhere. Machines were beeping all around him, and the room was dark. She couldn't believe this was the man she had been married to for two decades. He looked lifeless, pale and pathetic.

"Oh, Michael. I'm so sorry. I'm here now. You don't have to worry about anything but getting better," she said. The words she was saying were for the benefit of her daughters. She didn't want them to ever think that she hadn't done her best to keep their father alive.

"You're going to be okay. I'm going to make decisions for you, and I am going to do my best to get you healthy and well so you can get back to playing golf."

She knew, from looking at him, that the odds were he would never play golf again. He looked so broken, like the pieces of him could never be put back together. But, she knew that doctors could be miracle workers, and Michael had to want to get better for himself.

She spent the next hour talking to him, reminiscing, occasionally holding his hand when she could bring herself to do so. When she heard the door open, she assumed it was another nurse coming in for the constant round of vitals being checked or blood being drawn.

Instead, she saw Victoria.

She was standing there, her long hair pulled up into a ponytail. Her make-up was perfect, she held a designer handbag and was wearing jeans and a white T-shirt. She looked like a freaking supermodel.

"What are you doing here?" Victoria asked, crossing her arms.

"They called me because I am still legally his wife."

"I see. That's unfortunate."

"Well, from what I hear from the staff at the hospital, you don't seem very interested in taking care of him."

Victoria walked closer. "They shouldn't have told you that."

"Well, they did. And, despite the fact that he's treated me

poorly and opted instead to make his life with you, I honor my marriage vows. In sickness and in health."

"Well then, I guess you should know that I came here to tell him goodbye."

Julie stood up and quickly walked closer to Victoria. "Keep your voice down. He can hear you."

"I can't do this."

"You can't do what? You agreed to marry him and take vows."

"I'm not cut out for this. The doctors have told me he will have months, if not years, of rehab, and he probably will never be the same again. He might not be able to speak. He may not be able to walk. I can't do that. I live an active life-style. I'm sorry, but this is not the life I want for myself or my son."

"And how are you going to explain to your son one day that you abandoned his father in the hospital when he needed you most?"

"I guess I will have to cross that bridge when I come to it."

Julie shook her head. Never had she wanted to punch somebody as much as she did in that moment. And she was well aware of the fact that the woman she wanted to punch was her husband's mistress. Why did she feel so protective over Michael? He certainly hadn't felt protective over her.

"Don't you dare go over there and tell that man that you're leaving. It may cause him to give up. And he can't give up because he has two grown daughters that are depending on having their father to walk them down the aisle one day."

"Fine. When, or if, he ever comes to, please tell him that I'm sorry. Maybe I'm not a big enough person to take care of someone like this."

"You're a narcissist. You should look that up in the dictio-nary. I'm pretty sure your face will be next to it."

Victoria grunted and then turned around and walked out

of the hospital room. Julie truly hoped that would be the last time she ever saw that woman again.

Over the next twenty-four hours, Julie made every decision for Michael as he lay there, helpless. She sent Janine to stay at a local hotel while she tended to everything her husband needed. The doctors did another surgery, trying to repair his pelvis in a way that would allow him to walk again. They weren't sure. They said rehabilitation would be his best friend, and that a lot of it would depend on whether he really wanted to get better or not.

Still, Michael was unconscious. She had no idea if he knew she was there or not. She finally called her daughters and tried her best to explain what had happened. Both of them have been reduced to tears on the phone, wanting to fly to Boston and see their dad.

Julie had insisted they stay put for now. She felt like he was stable at the moment, and she really didn't want them to see him this way. Plus, getting Meg all the way back across the ocean by herself would only give Julie more anxiety and worries.

She felt so lonely sitting in the hospital. Every time she looked at him, she both wanted to hug him and punch him. Wanted to scream at him for ruining their life together. Right now, they could've been living together in a beach house somewhere, starting to enjoy the fruits of all those years of labor.

Instead, she had been forced to fly to take care of the man who had cheated on her and got another woman pregnant. She had been forced to defend his honor to the very same woman. None of it made any logical sense.

"Good afternoon, Mrs. Pike," Dr. Sadler said when making his rounds.

"Hi. Any update on his condition?"

"We think the surgery went fairly well. He has a long

recovery ahead of him. I don't want to be indelicate, but have you given any thought to how you're going to handle that? Will you move here from South Carolina?"

The thought had never dawned on her. She had made her life in Seagrove, and she had never had any intentions of leaving. But what would her daughters think if she continued her single life in her little island town and left their father out to dry?

"I don't know. This is all still really fresh."

"I understand. Well, let me know if you need anything. For now, I think he's stable."

"Do we know when he'll wake up?"

"No. That's really up to him." With that, Dr. Sadler walked out of the room, and Julie was left to wait and see when Michael would finally open his eyes.

~

JULIE DOZED in the chair beside Michael's bed. She had been there day after day, night after night. Through it all, she'd done video calls with her daughters and texted back and forth with Dawson about the house. Of course, Janine had spent many days with her in the hospital room, encouraging her to take breaks when she needed them.

As she sat there, she went through a range of emotions from sadness to resentfulness that Michael was still disrupting her life. She'd learned that the accident was caused by him falling asleep at the wheel on the way home from a business trip. How ironic that he was trying to get home to see Victoria, and she had abandoned him at the first sign of difficulty.

Night had descended over the city, and she looked out the window and noticed how different it was than night time in the Lowcountry. Gone were the sounds of bugs and waves crashing, and they were replaced by hospital monitors beeping and car horns on the road outside.

"Where... am... I?" She heard Michael say suddenly. Julie leapt to her feet and ran to the side of the bed.

"Michael, I'm here. It's Julie." She squeezed his hand lightly and stood over his face.

He squinted his eyes, trying to open them. "Victoria?"

Julie pushed her anger down. "No, Michael. It's me, Julie."

Again, he tried opening his eyes, the struggle on his face evident.

"Julie? Why are you here?"

Michael was so confused, and it pained her in a deeper way than she wanted to admit. Seeing her first love, her husband of over twenty years, struggle to understand why he was lying in a hospital bed, hooked to a bunch of machines, made her want to weep.

"Michael, I want you to stay calm, okay? You're in the hospital."

He opened his eyes further and looked around. Suddenly, he seemed distraught and scared. He began flailing his arms, trying in vain to get rid of the tubes and cords that were connected to his broken body.

"Michael, please, stay still. You can't do this..."

He continued pulling and then wincing in pain. In desperation, Julie finally pressed the button to call the nurse. She came quickly and asked Julie to leave the room while she attempted to settle him down.

Julie stepped into the hall, tears running down her face. This whole thing sucked in so many ways. She was being forced to care for the man who shattered her heart into a million pieces, yet he didn't want her there any more than he wanted her to remain his wife. He wanted Victoria.

She could walk away now. He was awake. He was alive.

She could just catch a flight and go back to the life she was building in Seagrove. Nobody would blame her.

Except maybe her daughters. She couldn't do that to them.

"What happened?" Janine said, as she ran toward her sister holding two coffee drinks.

"He woke up," Julie said. She wiped her face and attempted to channel her mother with her face of stone and lack of emotion.

"That's a good thing, right?"

"He doesn't understand where he is, and he wants Victoria, not me. Just like he wanted her for the last two years. I can't do this, Janine. How am I supposed to do this?"

Janine pulled her into a hug. "I know this is hard, sweetie. But, remember you're doing it for Meg and Colleen."

"I know that," Julie said, pulling back. "But, he doesn't want me."

"He's not in his right mind. Give it time. Think of it as a job you have to do. Like, what was the worst job you ever had?"

"I don't know," Julie said, taking a sip of her coffee.

"Come on, yes you do. We both know what it was."

Julie chuckled. "Cleaning toilets at McAffey's Chicken."

"Yes! That place was so gross. How long did you work there?"

"Three days," Julie said, letting out a loud laugh. "I couldn't get the smell of that food out of my jeans, so I burned them in Uncle Dan's backyard firepit!"

The two women giggled until they were interrupted by the nurse coming out of the room.

"How is he?" Julie asked.

"He's calmer now, but if he gets agitated again, press the button. We may have to sedate him."

"Thank you," Julie said. "Come with me?"

"Of course," Janine said.

They walked back into the room, but Janine stood in the doorway so Michael couldn't see her. They were never fans of each other, and she didn't want to upset him.

"Julie?" Michael said, still groggy.

"It's me. How are you feeling?"

"Tired. Sore. Confused. What happened to me? Why am I here?"

Julie sat down and tried her best to be calming. "You were in a car accident a few days ago."

"I've been here for days? But I don't remember anything."

"Michael, your injuries were very severe when you got here."

"Life threatening?"

"Yes. You've had two surgeries so far."

"So far?"

"I'm sure the doctor will come by soon and talk to you about your future rehab and prognosis."

"I'm scared, Julie."

Her heart ached. How she wished things could've been different for them. And now he was scared, and she wanted to comfort him the way a wife would comfort a husband. But she was all too aware that he didn't really want her. He just wanted someone.

"It's going to be okay, Michael. The doctors here are very experienced with this kind of thing."

He looked around. "Where's Victoria?"

Julie swallowed hard. What should she say? The last thing she wanted to do was upset him so much that he freaked out again. But, it was only a matter of time before he realized she wasn't there, and she wasn't coming.

"Um, I'm not sure where she is right now. You just need to focus on getting better. Meg and Colleen need their father."

"Meg and Colleen... are they here?"

"No. I asked them not to come until we know more about your rehab."

"Oh."

"Would you like to video chat with them? Maybe tomorrow when you're feeling up to it?"

"Yes. That would be good..." he said, his eyes starting to close.

"Sleep now, Michael. We'll talk more when you wake up, okay?"

"Okay..." he said, his voice drifting off as his eyes closed.

Julie slowly got up and exited the room, Janine trailing behind her.

"You amaze me, little sister," Janine said.

"That was hard. What am I supposed to say about the tramp?"

"I don't know. Maybe ask the doctor what to do?"

"Good idea. I think I'll go hunt him down. Listen, can you check in with Dawson? Make sure there's nothing he needs related to the house?"

"Sure."

Julie started walking up the hall, but turned back to her sister.

"Janine?"

"Yeah?"

"I just want you to know I love you."

Janine smiled. "I love you too, sis."

CHAPTER 14

*A*s the days wore on, Julie started to wonder if she would ever get back to Seagrove. Janine had stayed with her, but she'd finally encouraged her to go back to the cottage and help Dawson get things finished up on the renovation.

Michael had done video chats with Meg and Colleen, and he'd asked so many times about Victoria. For some reason, he didn't seem to comprehend that she wasn't coming back.

"You have to eat," Julie said as she watched him stare at a plate of Salisbury steak that didn't look appealing in the slightest.

"I'm not hungry," he grumbled. His personality had changed a lot. He was angry much of the time, his outbursts sometimes frightening her. The doctor said it was normal, but it was still hard to watch.

Rehab would begin soon now that his surgeries were over. Pain was a constant problem, and she wondered how he'd ever get off the pain medications they had him on. Then, she would remind herself that things needed to happen one step at a time.

"Michael, you can't rebuild your strength if you don't eat," she said as she stared at a magazine.

"Where is she?"

"Who?"

"Victoria."

"Let's not do this."

"Did you have her banned from the hospital? Is that your way of getting back at me?"

Julie was in shock. That was what he thought all this time? That she pushed her way into the hospital to take of him and banned his girlfriend?

"You must be joking."

"Joking? None of this is funny!" he yelled.

"Michael, hold your voice down," she whispered loudly.

"I want to see her."

Julie sighed. "Fine. I didn't want to tell you this until you were better, but Victoria bailed."

"What do you mean bailed?"

"Michael, she was only here for a short time right after your accident. By the time I arrived the next day, she had decided she didn't want to take care of you."

He stared at her for a long moment, his eyes knitted together. She couldn't tell if he was shocked or sad or angry. He just stared. It was like he couldn't comprehend her words.

"I don't believe you. Where's my phone?"

Again, Julie sighed, something she was doing a lot more lately. She walked across the room and dug into his jean's pocket. She pressed the button on his phone, which, of course, was dead.

"Your phone needs to be charged," she said, as she walked back to her seat and replaced her charging phone with his. As soon as his lit up, she noticed a picture of Victoria and their son was his screensaver. She wanted to vomit.

"I don't know what kind of game you're playing, Julie, but you won't break us up. I love her. And I love my son."

She'd had enough, and came out of her seat. "Look, Michael, I've tried to be nice! I've tried to maintain my composure because I love our daughters, and I want them to have their father. But, I can't do this anymore. Victoria told me to my face that she wasn't going to take care of you. She didn't want to be here. Heck, I don't want to be here, either, but for totally different reasons you can probably imagine. Call her all you want. Text her too. Send a skywriter. Whatever you need to do. But the woman bailed when you needed her, and I want to feel sorry for you, but you're making it incredibly difficult!"

She took in a deep breath and sat back down, avoiding eye contact with Michael. She could feel him looking at her, though.

"She left me?"

"She left you."

He didn't speak another word for several minutes. There was just a deafening silence in the room, the sound of beeping from his monitor was the only noise.

"I guess this is karma. You must be pretty happy."

She craned her head at him. "Seriously? What kind of person do you think I am?"

"I'm sorry," he said, softly. "Why did you come?"

"Because they called me."

"You could have said no. I wouldn't have blamed you."

She looked at him. "I'm here because of our daughters. Nothing more, trust me."

"I heard you live at the beach."

"I do."

"Do you like it there?"

"I love it there."

"Good. You deserve happiness, Julie."

She didn't say anything in return. She didn't care what he thought she deserved. She had what she thought was happiness until he decided to throw it all away.

"Thank you for being here. I'm sorry I assumed the worst in you. I think these meds are messing me up."

Before she could respond, the door opened. A receptionist from the lobby was standing there holding a large box.

"Is this Michael Pike's room?"

"Yes, it is," Julie said.

"I have a box for his wife. Is that you?"

Julie paused and cleared her throat. "I'm Julie."

"Great. This delivery came for you. Someone must really care about you," she said, smiling as she handed it over.

Julie was confused. She had no idea who would send her something.

"What is that?" Michael asked.

"I don't know." Julie sat the box on a rolling tray table and opened it as the receptionist left the room.

Inside were heated containers of food and a note.

Dear Julie,

We sure have missed you around here. I know you might be missing your new home too, so I called around until I found a decent Southern cooking restaurant in Boston. Jeez, those people don't even drink sweet tea! Can you imagine? Anyway, inside you'll find shrimp and grits, cornbread, fried okra and some peach cobbler. Won't be nearly as good as Lucy's, but we'll fill you up when you get back. Everybody's praying for you. Dixie said she misses you too. Come home soon!

Dawson

Her heart was pounding. No one had ever done something so nice for her. She wanted to go back to Seagrove even worse now. Struggling not to cry, she folded the letter back up and put it in her pocket.

"What is that smell?" Michael asked, waving a hand in front of his face.

"Food," she said, dryly.

"Who sent it?"

"My friend back in Seagrove."

"What's her name?"

"Dawson."

"A woman named Dawson?" he said with a laugh.

Julie turned and looked at him. "I never said it was a woman."

Michael's face fell a bit, and Julie almost let out a giggle. But, now wasn't the time to rub it in his face that she had a new life and a new male friend. After all, nothing romantic was going on with Dawson.

"Oh," he said. She expected him to ask more questions, but he didn't. "Smells bad."

Julie rolled her eyes. "Then I'll take it down to the cafeteria. I need to get a drink anyway."

Michael said nothing as she took her purse and her bag of food and headed down the hallway.

After finding a table and setting up her meal, she dialed Dawson's number on video chat.

"Hey there! Long time, no see!" he said, a big smile on his face. She could see the marsh behind him, and it made her miss the wild place she now called home.

"Thank you so much for the food!" She turned the phone around so he could see it on the table.

"Oh, you got it! Good. Those Northerners thought I was some kind of hillbilly nutcase asking for sweet tea," he said with a laugh.

"I bet. I am going to greatly enjoy this food, though. Hospital food and subs from the corner store just aren't cutting it anymore."

"I hear Janine is on her way back?"

"Yeah. No need for her to be stuck here too. I think Michael is out of the woods for now."

"So you're coming back soon too?"

She paused. "I can't. His supposed fiancee abandoned him. Literally said she couldn't take care of a disabled person who would need rehab for months or years."

"Wow. She sounds like a piece of work."

"Yep. So, I'm his next of kin. I just can't leave him. My daughters would never forgive me."

"I get it. Take care of yourself."

"Thanks, Dawson," she said, waving at the screen before ending their call. She felt a sense of homesickness once they hung up. As she took her first bite of the shrimp and grits, she closed her eyes and imagined sitting on her bench near the marsh.

~

DR. SADLER POINTED to the X-ray on the screen. "We were able to repair the pelvic bone, but rehab is going to be crucial to your recovery, Mr. Pike. You'll need to be diligent and work hard to get back full mobility."

"When can I leave this place?" Michael asked. He was growing more irritated by the day. Over three weeks in the hospital had made him frustrated and angry at his body and the entire medical community. Julie had tried to tell him that they'd saved his life, but he didn't seem phased enough not to snap at every doctor and nurse in the place.

"Actually, that's what I wanted to talk to you about. We've set up a rigorous rehab schedule for you. Everything will be done here at the hospital in our outpatient wing."

"So, I can go home?"

"That depends on whether you have someone to care for you. You'll need someone to bring you to your appointments and so forth because you'll be in a wheelchair for quite some time."

Julie suddenly felt sick and lightheaded. Realizing that she was the person expected to do all of this, she wracked her brain, trying to figure out a way that she could go home sooner rather than later.

"Can we hire a private nurse to do this?" she asked the doctor, well aware that Michael was looking at her. "I live in South Carolina."

"You could, potentially. But my insurance lady here at the hospital tells me Michael doesn't have coverage for that sort of thing. That would be out of pocket, and, frankly, it would be quite expensive. We're talking about months of rehab."

"Could he stay in the hospital and receive rehab here?" she was grasping at straws now.

"Unfortunately, that's not an option. His insurance coverage wouldn't provide for something like that either." The doctor looked between them and seemed to sense he needed to leave the room. "Why don't I give you two a chance to talk. I'll be back around later this evening."

Once he'd walked out, Julie stood and stared out the window. The city was so far removed from her life back in Seagrove. So much hustle and bustle.

"Julie?"

"Yeah?"

"You're not thinking of leaving me, are you?"

"What?"

"Leaving me."

"Michael, you already left me months ago."

"No, I mean, you're going to stay and help me, aren't you? I don't have anyone else here."

She knew she should feel bad for him, but all she felt was resentfulness, How could he ask for more from her?

"Michael, I have a life and a job back in Seagrove. I can't stay here for months."

He leaned his head back against the pillow and looked at the ceiling. "I'm sorry for what I did."

"What do you mean?"

"I'm sorry for cheating on you. I don't know what I was thinking."

"It doesn't matter now. We're divorced."

"Almost, but it's not official yet."

"What are you getting at?"

He looked at her. "Maybe this is a sign."

"A sign of what?" She sat back down and looked at him.

"Maybe we needed this time together. Maybe we can get things back on track."

She knew he was saying it out of desperation, but still a part of her wondered if he meant it.

"Let's not do this."

"I'm being serious. Laying in a hospital bed for three weeks gives you plenty of time to think. I see my mistakes, and I see what an incredible woman you are to come here and take care of the man who broke your heart."

"I had no choice, Michael. But you're alive, and I can't stay here and lose myself again. You'll need to work this out for yourself, as a newly single man."

"What will our girls think if you leave me?" Now, the real Michael was showing up. He didn't want her; he just didn't want to be alone and helpless.

"Don't you dare try to guilt me, Michael Pike! Do you have any idea what it took for me to come here and care for you? I left my new job, my new home…"

"Really? From what I hear, your home is a pit."

She wanted to punch him, but somehow that seemed inappropriate to slug a helpless man in a hospital bed.

"I'm going to take a walk before I say something I might

regret," she said, grabbing her jacket and heading outside into the cool October air.

She stood outside of the hospital and sucked in a deep breath. What was she going to do? How would she ever get back to Seagrove?

"Hello?" She said as she pulled her ringing phone from her pocket.

"Hey, Mom," Meg said from the other end of the line.

"Sweetie, so good to hear from you! How are you?"

"Worried about Daddy most of the time."

"He's doing just fine. In fact, the doctor is releasing him soon. He'll need to come back for rehab, of course, but he's going home."

"Oh, that's great! Will he be in a wheelchair?"

"Yes, for a long time."

"I feel so bad for him. At least he has you. I'm so glad you're there, Mom. I know it must be hard, but I want you to know how much me and Colleen appreciate what you're doing."

Julie pushed back her tears. She wasn't crying for Michael. She was crying for her girls and their fear of losing their father. And, if she was honest with herself, she was crying over the fact that she was about to lose everything she'd built all over again. And Michael was at the root of all of it.

"I'm just doing what has to be done," Julie said, trying to sound positive. "I know your Dad will be fine no matter what."

Meg paused for a moment. "But, you will stay with him, won't you?"

"Yes, honey, of course, I will. For as long as it takes."

And then the tears silently fell down her face while she listened to Meg catch her up on life across the pond.

~

CARING for someone so debilitated by injury was almost more than Julie could handle, but when it was the man she resented most in the world, it was even harder.

"How was physical therapy?" she asked, as they pulled away from the hospital for what seemed like the millionth time already.

"Same as always. Painful."

"Do you want to drive through and get some food?"

"Don't you ever cook anymore?" Michael grumbled.

"I'm a little busy these days, if you haven't noticed."

"Well, I'm getting tired of burgers and fries."

"Noted," she said, rolling her eyes as she drove. Her phone rang from the cup holder, so she picked it up when they were safely stopped in traffic. "Hello?"

"Hey there."

"Dawson, so good to hear from you. How is everyone?" Julie said. Out of the corner of her eye, she could see Michael rolling his eyes.

"Good. We all miss having you around. Any update on coming back?"

"No, not yet. How's the house coming along?"

"It's almost finished. Just need you here to make some final design decisions."

"Yeah, I don't know when that would be. Can Janine help?"

"She said she doesn't want to chance messing it up," he said, with a laugh.

"That's probably smart," Julie said. "Maybe we can video chat later, and you can show me some things?"

"Sounds good. How about around six?"

"I'll be waiting for your call."

She ended the call and started driving again. Michael was unusually quiet.

"So, you're dating this guy?"

"That's none of your business."

"I've been married to you a long time. I think it is my business if my wife is dating another man."

Enraged, Julie pulled into a parking lot and stopped the car. She turned to him. "You're kidding, right?"

"No, I'm not kidding. You barely know this person, right?"

"Again, my personal life is none of your business."

He sighed. "Julie, I thought we were going to try to make this work."

"What?"

"I told you that I thought my accident might be a sign that we need to try again. Hearing you talk to that Dawson guy just made me realize how much I don't want you to move on without me."

Oh, how she would've loved to have heard that a few months ago. But, when he said it, she felt nothing that resembled love. She felt pity, resentment and frustration. She felt obligation most of all.

"Michael, I'm sorry, but our marriage is over. Me taking care of you is for the benefit of our daughters, but it doesn't mean anything about our relationship."

"You can't mean that, Jules. We had two decades together. You don't just throw that away," he said, looking at her and trying to touch her hand. She glared at him.

"You threw it away first."

"You're right, and I'm sorry. I know I hurt you. But, I know what I did wrong now. I'm willing to get therapy to be a better man. I'll do anything to make this work again."

"No, Michael. I'm not leaving my new life in Seagrove."

"Then what if I come there?"

"What?"

"I'll move there. I can do rehab anywhere, right? And we can work on building our relationship. Can you imagine how excited the girls would be?"

All she heard was that he was willing to go to Seagrove. Even if she didn't want to get back together, it would make life a lot easier if he came home with her. Of course, Janine might kill him in his sleep, but that was a bridge she'd cross later.

"So, you'd agree to come to Seagrove and live?"

"I would do anything for you, Jules," he said, his voice lower. Ugh. It made her sick to think he wanted her again. For some reason, she didn't see him that way anymore. A part of her felt guilty for pretending they'd have any chance of ever getting back together, but the larger part of her wanted to get back to her home on the marsh.

And, as her daughter once told her, "Players deserve to get played". She probably wasn't referring to her father, though.

"Okay."

"Okay?" Michael asked, his eyes wide.

"Let's talk to your doctors about moving your treatment program to Charleston."

He smiled broadly. "Thank you, Julie. You won't regret this."

"Michael, this doesn't mean anything has changed."

"But, there's hope, and that's enough for now."

She didn't respond, and instead pulled back into traffic, thinking of how excited she was to see Dawson, Dixie and Janine again.

CHAPTER 15

*I*t had taken a lot longer than she expected to get the doctors to approve Michael's move. Four more weeks had passed, and Julie was getting antsy. Talking to Dawson over video chat about the house wasn't nearly as fun as being there in person to pick out her home decor.

She could see the cottage transforming before her eyes, and it made her ache for Seagrove. She couldn't believe how it felt like home to her, like she'd been there her whole life.

"We leave tomorrow?"

"Yes. And the real estate agent will have the condo listed by this weekend," Julie said as she packed her suitcase.

"Oh. Good." Michael's voice was different. He didn't sound excited, which was odd given how much he'd pushed for the move and the prospect of them getting back together.

Meg and Colleen had both been so excited to hear they were moving in together even though Julie had tried to make them understand it didn't mean anything.

"I think your phone is ringing," Michael said, rolling his eyes. He was tired of her talking to all of her Seagrove friends, and he made no secret about it.

Julie walked to her phone and saw Dixie's number. "Hey, Dixie!"

"Hey yourself!" Dixie said, her Southern accent a sweet sound to Julie's ear.

She waved at Michael to say she was stepping outside to take the call and then went onto the balcony overlooking the city, sliding the door shut behind her.

"So, what's going on?"

"Dawson tells me you're bringing your husband back to Seagrove?"

Julie sighed. "It was the only way I was ever getting home."

"Honey, I know this isn't my business, and you can tell me to shut my trap if you want, but I don't think this is a very good idea."

"I don't either, but my daughters would never forgive me if I didn't take care of their father."

"Your daughters are grown women. Surely, they'd understand that you can't spend the rest of your life caring for the man who betrayed you."

"I feel obligated. At least this way I can be home and have ya'll around me."

"Scoundrels rarely change, ya know?"

"I know."

"And you deserve this new life you've built."

"Thank you, Dixie. And I appreciate it."

"He'll show you who he really is again. Promise me when he does that you'll finally let yourself break away and not feel obligated to this man, okay? Pay attention. Don't let guilt cause you to waste your life."

She appreciated Dixie's words more than she could describe, especially since her own mother was little help in situations like these. Her only advice had been to try to work it out because Michael would go back to work one day, and she'd be supported again.

"I'll pay attention. I promise."

"Well, I've got a customer coming in. Love you, sweetie."

"Love you too, Dixie. See ya soon."

She pressed end and looked out over the city. Although it was lovely, she couldn't wait to hear the sounds of the marsh again. She turned to go back into the condo, but she could hear Michael talking softly. Quietly, she tip toed to the bedroom door and listened.

"I know, honey... It's a long way... But as soon as I get well, I'm coming back... I miss you both so much... Yeah, I get why you couldn't take care of me... I know it was too much, Victoria...I don't blame you... I love you..."

Julie seethed with rage. She grabbed her purse and stormed out of the condo, slamming the door behind her.

~

MICHAEL BLEW up her phone with calls and texts, but Julie had ignored them for hours. When she finally came back to the condo, he was sitting in his wheelchair, staring at the door.

"Where did you go? You had me scared to death. I needed to go to the bathroom, and you weren't here to help me!"

She laughed. "Why don't you call Victoria?"

"What?"

"Do you think I'm hard of hearing?"

He swallowed. "You heard me?"

"Yep. And thank God I did," she walked to her suitcase and zipped it up.

"Where are you going?"

"Home."

"What? You can't just leave me here!" He followed her around the room in his wheelchair.

"I can, and I will. You see, I just spoke to your therapists, and they've arranged transportation to your appointments for you. They've also set up an intern to come by a couple of times a day to help you. I called the real estate agent and cancelled the listing. And, most importantly, I called your daughters and told them why I was leaving."

"You told them?"

"Yep," she said, gathering up her make-up and putting into her carryon bag.

"That wasn't fair, Julie."

She stopped and looked at him. "You know what isn't fair, Michael? Having your husband of twenty one years cheat on you, get another woman pregnant, get engaged to her, get in an accident and then expect the very same wife to fix you back up so you can be with your skank again. That's what isn't fair."

"Look, Victoria called me a few days ago and apologized. She's just not cut out for caregiving like you are. But, if you want me to stop talking to her, I will. I think counseling could help us…"

"Stop!" she said, putting her hand in the air. "Look, I don't know what's happened to the man I married, but he isn't here anymore. I've already grieved that loss. I feel nothing when I look at you. I thank God that I heard that call because it finally shook some sense into me. You're not my responsibility anymore. I deserve to have a life I love because I built one. Goodbye, Michael."

"You can't do this, Julie," he said, following her to the door. "You know this is wrong."

"Call the doctor's office if you need anything. Oh, and I asked your mother to come for a visit."

"My mother? But, she'll drive me crazy!"

Julie turned and smiled. "I know."

~

JULIE HADN'T TOLD anyone she was coming. She wanted it to be a surprise. As she pulled into her driveway, she let out the breath she'd been holding for so long. Home.

She walked in the front door and was shocked when she saw how perfect it all was. The paint, the furniture, the floors. It was better than she could've ever imagined.

"Sis?" Janine said from the hallway. She ran to her and gave her a big hug, something she'd have never thought possible a few months ago.

"It's me!" Julie said, her voice muffled by Janine's curly mane of hair.

"Where's the idiot?"

"In Boston."

"What happened?"

"He showed his true colors again. Wanted me to help him get better and then go back to Victoria. So, I left him."

"I'm so proud of you!"

"The girls understood, which surprised me. So, that gave me the strength to leave and come back home. And this place looks amazing! Where's Dawson?"

"He's down by the marsh eating his lunch, I think. And I know he can't wait to see you. I think he has a little crush."

Julie rolled her eyes. "No, he doesn't."

"Okay, whatever you say..." she said as she walked back up the hallway.

Julie put down her bags and walked out the back door. She could see Dawson sitting on the bench, her favorite place on her property. He was eating a sandwich and looking out over the marsh grass waving in the breeze. She sucked in a deep breath of the musky marsh smell, and it smelled like home.

"Hey," she said softly as she walked up to him. He dropped

his sandwich and shot up off the bench, a huge smile on his face.

"Oh my gosh, you're back!"

Dawson pulled her into a bear hug, and she melted into a puddle. Oh crap, she had a crush on him too. Did forty-somethings even have crushes?

It felt good to have someone hold her tightly again. She pressed her cheek into his chest, drinking in the moment. He smelled like home.

Dawson cleared his throat and stepped back, running his fingers through his hair. "Sorry about that. I wasn't thinking."

"It's okay. I didn't mind."

They stared at each other for a moment. "At the risk of sounding very non macho, can I just say that I missed you?"

"I missed you too," she said, her face burning.

"Where's your husband?"

"In Boston."

Dawson cocked his head. "But, I thought…"

"This is my new beginning, and I'm going to protect it. So, he's not coming here."

He smiled. "Good. I thought that was a very bad idea."

"That's what Dixie said too. Listen, I just want to thank you for taking care of my place while I was gone. It looks amazing."

"It was my pleasure."

"I was wondering if I could take you to dinner sometime as a way to say thank you?"

He smiled that crooked smile. "Why, are you asking me on a date, Julie?"

"What would you say if I was?"

"I would say what time should I pick you up?"

Yes, life on the island was turning out much better than she expected. Maybe new beginnings are bumpy, but so worth it.

C hristmas was Julie's favorite time of the year, and having dinner at her new house was even more exciting. She and Janine had had way too much fun decorating the place, with Dawson's help, of course.

The three of them had found the biggest Christmas tree they could, carting it in his truck back to the cottage. Thank goodness for high ceilings or the thing might have popped through the roof.

Julie had convinced her mother and her husband, Buddy, to come to Seagrove for the holidays. SuAnn had argued a little, but when Janine had sent her some pictures of the cottage, all new and renovated, she finally caved.

The best part of Fall had been the budding relationship between Dawson and Julie. They were taking things very slowly and had only been on a few dates, although most evenings Dawson was around, fixing this or that in her house. Nothing really needed to be done, but he seemed to find things to do anyway.

Now that the divorce was final, Julie knew she could date, but she'd been hesitant, wanting to protect her heart from being shattered again. Not that Dawson would ever do that. He just wasn't the type. But, then again, she never imagined Michael would do what he did.

Although Julie was glad to have Dawson, Janine, Dixie, her mother and Buddy at the house for the holidays, she missed her daughters. Colleen had a huge case to work on and just couldn't get enough time off for the cross country trip. Meg was all the way in Europe, and coming home for Christmas just wasn't in the cards.

"I'm glad you and Buddy could make it," Julie said to her mother as they prepared the salad.

"Me too, dear. And this place looks lovely. Dawson did a wonderful job getting it in shape."

Julie smiled. "So you don't fear for my life anymore?"

"Well, I wouldn't say that. This island is a bit remote for my taste."

"Oh, Mother, drink some wine and loosen up," Janine said as she walked into the kitchen. She handed her mother a glass and laughed.

"By the way, do you remember awhile back, when you gave me that medical power of attorney in case I needed to make decisions for you?" Julie asked SuAnn.

"Yes, of course. Why?"

"Well, Mom, I called your doctor a few days ago."

"Why would you do that?"

"Because you've been so tight lipped about your medical problem, and we were worried about you. Imagine my surprise when I found out the blood work you had us scared about was simply high cholesterol."

SuAnn smiled. "A mother has to use whatever she can to get her daughters back together. I regret nothing," she said, taking a sip of her wine.

Janine and Julie laughed and put their arms around each other. "I guess it all worked out," Julie said.

"Yeah. But, don't lie to us again. I was really worried."

"Can I help with anything?" Dawson asked, as he walked into the kitchen. Julie thought he looked especially yummy today with his red plaid shirt, distressed jeans and his cowboy boots. Like a sexy lumberjack.

"You can take the ham to the table, if you don't mind," Julie said, smiling up at him. They were going on another date soon. The New Year's Eve Island Bash was coming up, and even people from the mainland came to that. She was hoping for a big New Year's kiss.

"Sure," he said, winking at her as he picked up the ham and walked to the table.

"My, my, my," SuAnn said. "Somebody is quite smitten with you."

"And I'm pretty smitten with him," Julie admitted. "But, we're going slow."

"Smart move," Janine said.

"Don't go so slow that you lose him, dear. You're getting older, and the pickings get slimmer," SuAnn said.

"Oh, Mom. Come on, let's leave Julie in peace," Janine said, guiding her mother away from the kitchen.

"Merry Christmas!" Dixie said as she walked up to Julie. She had obviously been waiting for SuAnn to leave the kitchen. They weren't fans of each other.

Julie hugged her. "Merry Christmas! I'm so glad you could be here."

"Thanks for inviting me. The house looks beautiful. Dawson did a great job here."

"Yes, he did."

"You okay? You seem a little sad."

"I miss my girls. I've never had Christmas without them."

"I understand."

"Oh, I'm sorry, Dixie. I know you must miss your boys too."

"I do. But, some things can't be fixed, no matter how hard you try."

"Never give up hope."

"You know, you're like the daughter I never had."

Julie smiled. "Thank you. And you're like the mother I always wanted," she whispered.

Dixie laughed at that. "Did you hear a knock at the door?"

"Is that what that was? It's so loud in here." Julie walked across the room and opened the door. Standing there was a man, close to her age, with dark brown hair. He looked angry or constipated, or maybe both. "Can I help you?"

"I'm looking for Dixie," he said, his tone sharp and cold.

"Um, okay..." Julie said, opening the door a bit wider. Dixie appeared behind her. Julie heard her gasp a bit.

"William?"

"Hello, Mom."

Julie realized this wasn't going to be a normal Christmas dinner, after all.

CPSIA information can be obtained
at www.ICGtesting.com
Printed in the USA
BVHW040211220623
666248BV00004B/136